The Discovery
of Chocolate

The Discovery
of Chocolate

James Runcie

W F HOWES LTD

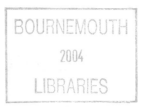

This large print edition published in 2002 by
W F Howes Ltd
Units 6/7, Victoria Mills, Fowke Street
Rothley, Leicester LE7 7PJ

1 3 5 7 9 10 8 6 4 2

First published in 2001 by HarperCollins*Publishers*

ISBN 1 84197 521 4

Typeset by Palimpsest Book Production Limited,
Polmont, Stirlingshire
Printed and bound in Great Britain
by Antony Rowe Ltd, Chippenham, Wilts.

for Marilyn

CHAPTER 1

Although it is true that I have been considered lunatic on many occasions in the last five hundred years, it must be stated, at the very beginning of this sad and extraordinary tale, that I have been most grievously misunderstood. The elixir of life was drunk in all innocence and my dog had nothing to do with it.

Let me explain.

Having once embarked on a precarious and often dangerous quest, I have now been condemned to roam the world, unable to die. I have lost all trace of my friends and family and have been separated from the only woman that I have ever loved. And although it might seem a blessing to be given the possibility of eternal life and to taste its delights without end, taking pleasure where one will and living without judgement or morality, it is, in fact, an existence of unremitting purgatory. I cannot believe that this has happened to me and have only decided to tell my story so that others who might seek to cheat death and live such a life should be alert to its dangers.

My troubles began at the age of twenty when I,

1

Diego de Godoy, notary to the Emperor Charles V, first crossed the Atlantic as a young man in search of fame and fortune. The year was fifteen hundred and eighteen.

Of course it was all for love.

Isabella de Quintallina, a lady of sixteen years who lived, like me, in Seville, had taken possession of my soul. Although our temperaments seemed ideally suited, my lack of noble birth put me at a considerable disadvantage, and, after six months of prolonged and ardent courtship, I began to doubt if I could ever win her love. I was further dismayed when Isabella set me the following challenge.

If we were to be joined in matrimony, I would have to hazard everything I owned – all my prospects, all my safety and all my future – on one bold venture. She asked me to travel with the conquistadors, and return, not only with the gold and riches on which our future life together would depend, but also with a gift which no man or woman had ever received before, a true and secret treasure which only we would share. Isabella had heard that in the New World gold and silver could be plucked from the earth in abundance. Pepper, nutmegs and cloves could be harvested in all seasons; cinnamon had been found within the bark of a tree; and strange insects could render up vibrant tints to dye her silks the deepest scarlet. She was convinced that I would be able to find a love token that was both spectacular and unique, and would wait for me for two years, suffering the attentions of no other man, until the arrival of her eighteenth birthday. Succeed, and Isabella vowed the world would be mine; if I failed, however, she would have no choice but to seek the hand of another and never look upon me again.

Two years! This was more than all the time in which we had known one another.

Despair entered the very fabric of my being, and I do not think that I had ever felt so alone. My sweet mother had died when I was an infant, and my poor blind father was too distressed to counsel me, terrified that I would never return from such a journey.

But there was no choice.

I must live or die for love.

After presenting me with her portrait in a miniature silver case, Isabella took pity on my plight and gave me her pet greyhound to act as a companion on the long voyage ahead. Tears welled up in her eyes, the hound whimpered in accompaniment, and my beloved implored me to see the sacrifice she had made, asking me to believe that such generosity surely proved her love, since there was nothing she valued more in the world than Pedro's devoted and unquestioning loyalty.

This was extremely awkward because, in truth, I did not actually want the dog. I have always detested the manner in which such animals fawn upon their owners, bite the heels of strangers, soil gardens, and rut at the most inopportune moments. But this young puppy was forced into my arms without any suspicion that he might be the last thing in the world that I required. In short, I was landed with him, and could only declare that he was indeed the true testament of her love, and that I would endeavour to return with an equivalent prize.

And so, after a tearful and prolonged farewell with my father, I took my leave. Isabella threw herself into my arms, pressing her breasts against my chest, her blonde ringlets falling on my shoulders, and then watched from the quayside as I boarded the caravel *Santa Gertrudis*. Great cries of '*A Dios, a Dios*' rose from the ship, and the crowds called out, '*Buen viaje, buen viaje*'. Slowly, and with a terrible inevitability, the ship pulled away and the sight of my beloved began to recede into the distance. It was as if we were being stretched apart from each other for ever. I clasped Isabella's portrait to my bosom and felt a great weight behind my eyes as the tears welled up. All that had previously defined me was swept away by the journey down the Guadalquivir River and out to sea towards the Americas.

I had never before contemplated the life of a sailor, and the inconstancy of the voyage disheartened me, for there was not a moment when our ship was still or we could be at peace. The calm seas which we met at the outset of the journey were interrupted by unwelcome and intemperate gusts of wind, and strange currents pulled the ship in directions in which we had not meant to travel. The nights were filled with the fearsome sounds of dragging, moaning and creaking, deep in the hull. Horses neighed below, pigs moved amidst the straw, and rats scuttled past us as we cleaned cannon, arranged sails, and washed down the deck.

But after we had passed Las Islas Canarias we found calm seas and winds in our favour. We sailed as on a river of fresh water, taking much delight in fishing for the glittering dorado that we ate each evening. Pedro ran upon the deck, and even on one occasion swam in the sea, the sailors cheering his adventure, until he lost his confidence and required rescue. Of course it fell to me, as his new owner, to dive in and save him. I dared not think how many fathoms deep the ocean ran beneath us and I was nearly drowned bringing him back on board. But my act of mercy only served to make the hound love me all the more, and I found his dogged devotion so all-encompassing that I believed that I would never enjoy a moment alone for the rest of my life.

He was a permanent reminder of Isabella, to whom all thoughts returned, like doves at nightfall. Each evening I lay on my hammock with her portrait in my hand and Pedro asleep at my feet, dreaming of the nights that I would one day spend with my beloved rather than her accursed dog. Even in the daytime I found myself quite lost in the memory of her beauty, and I was reprimanded that I should concentrate on my tasks and become more of a man and less of a dreamer.

I steeled myself to concentrate on my duties, but was surprised to find that all seamen were expected to sew. Although this seemed an effeminate occupation, it was taken extremely seriously, and I discovered that the neatest hem-stitchers were even given extra rations, the task of patching and making sails being considered so vital to the success of our endeavours. I was detailed to pick old rope apart and then re-use it to make ladders, or ratlines, by which our men were able to scramble to points aloft. I subsequently found myself spending many hours on deck involved in their construction, proving so adept at the task that I was soon promoted to making lanyards and shroud stays.

After seven weeks, we landed in Cuba.

It was the feast of the Epiphany, fifteen hundred and nineteen. I had expected it to be winter, but the air was filled with the sweet scents of tamarind and jacaranda, hibiscus and bougainvillea. This was, indeed, a New World.

At noon the next day we met the Governor of the islands, Diego de Velázquez, who had been in these lands some five years. He bid us welcome and informed us that our arrival was timely: there was an expedition underway to discover new territories a few weeks hence, led by one Hernán Cortés.

Of good stature, broad-shouldered and deep-chested, with fair, almost reddish hair, worn long and with a beard, Cortés possessed neither patience nor self-doubt. He determined to use my skills as a notary, and asked me to record every detail of his journey to the Americas, issuing declarations, recording confessions and sending accurate *relaciones* back to Spain. I would also be called upon to write out and proclaim new oaths of allegiance to Queen Doña Juana and her son, the Emperor Charles V, made by the *caciques*, or leaders, of the realms that we would surely conquer.

And so it was that on the tenth of February fifteen hundred and nineteen, just after Mass, I, Diego de Godoy, and my over-eager dog, Pedro the greyhound, boarded the lateen-rigged caravel *San Sebastián* and began to sail along the coast of Yucatán in the company of ten other ships under the leadership of the aforementioned Cortés. Diego de Velázquez attempted to recall us from the journey at the very last minute, questioning the legitimate authority of Cortés to colonise further lands without the consent of His Majesty, but our General was in no mood to turn back. The adventure had begun, and I now found myself in the company of friends upon whose abilities my life would come to depend: Antonio de Villaroel, the standard-bearer; Anton de Alaminos, the pilot; Aguilar, the interpreter; Maestre Juan, the surgeon; Andres Nuñez, the boat-builder; Alonso Yañez, the carpenter; together with some thirty-two crossbowmen, thirteen musketeers, ten gunners, six harquebusiers, two blacksmiths, and, to keep us hearty, Ortiz, the musician, and Juan, the harpist, from Valencia.

Hernán Cortés may have been an irascible commander, quick to find fault with people in his charge, but his ways were softened by his devoted companion Doña Marina, the daughter of a Mexican *cacique*, whom he had been given in the province of Tabasco. A most comely woman, with long dark hair, golden skin and deep brown eyes, Doña Marina had a natural authority. She also seemed unwilling to wear a corset, preferring loose and revealing clothing which fell easily from her body, exposing areas of soft and rounded flesh that were the very essence of temptation. She possessed the most sensual of walks: lilting and slow, with her body arched back and her breasts held high, as if she was quite accustomed to being the most beautiful person wherever she went.

I must confess that I found her disarmingly attractive, and soon could not stop myself thinking about her. Courteous and calm, Doña Marina was someone I needed to befriend, since she and Aguilar were the only people who could speak the native tongue of Nahuatl, and I was certain that I would need her aid if I was to fulfil my quest.

Sailing off the coast of Cempaola, we were greeted in a friendly fashion by some forty Indians in large dugout canoes. They had pierced holes in their lips and ears, and had inserted either pieces of gold or lapis. This jewellery glinted in the light, and both their nakedness and their beauty amazed me. They shouted, '*Lope luzio, Lope luzio,*' and pulled up alongside our ships, offering fine cotton garments, war clubs, axes and necklaces. As they prepared to climb aboard, one of them stumbled and let fall from his pack into the sea a handful of what appeared to be dried brown almonds, and became much distressed. Nobody could see clearly what these articles were, but others began to check that they had not done the same, looking about their bodies for these strange dark objects, and counting them in their hands. The leader of the sailors then climbed aboard with several of his officials, and began to point at the land ahead, as if encouraging our men to go there. After weighing anchor, our camp was established on the shore, while I proceeded with Cortés and thirty soldiers to meet the local *cacique*, and to begin my written record of our adventures.

The chieftain at Cempaola was the fattest person I had ever seen. He was bare-chested, and an enormous expanse of flesh hung over his skirt and sandals, as if he were nothing less than a man mountain of lard and gold. Making a deep bow to Cortés, he then ordered that a *petaca*, or chest, filled with beautiful and richly worked golden objects – necklaces, bracelets, rings, cloaks and skirts – be placed before us. No one had ever seen such treasure before; there were mirrors set with garnets, bracelets of lapis, a helmet of stained mosaic and a maniple of wolfskin. The chest alone would surely have made a man's fortune, but we were careful to seem unmoved by our first true glimpse of undreamed wealth.

The *cacique* then unfurled ten bales of the purest white linen, embroidered with gold feathers. I immediately thought that this could have made the most glorious gown for Isabella and would have delved into my knapsack to offer my paltry goods in exchange had I been a more esteemed member of the party. But Cortés had forbidden any of us to converse with the *cacique*. He alone was to be the Master of Ceremonies, producing clear, green and twisted Spanish beads, as well as two exquisite holland shirts and a long-piled Flemish hat in return for these new treasures.

The citizens of Cempaola were amazed both by our armour and by our appearance, and now asked if we had come from the east, since, according to their religion, the god of the fifth sun was expected at any moment. Perhaps we were angels, or divine messengers?

Cortés now began to tell the Cempaolans of our Christian belief. He explained that they must accept our faith and cleanse their souls of sin, trusting in the promises of our Saviour, Jesus Christ, who had been sent by God to redeem us from death and grant us eternal life.

Bartolomé de Olmedo, the Mercedarian friar, now ordered that the whole town should take part in a Mass of Thanksgiving. The Cempaolans were given new Spanish names after the saints of our Church and christened in an enormous candle-lit ceremony. Eight Indian girls were then presented to the captains of our ships, who took them away for an altogether different kind of baptism.

One of the girls walked up to me and touched my beard (which I had grown in an attempt to look swarthy). She wore a short skirt, but her chest was naked, and as she caressed my face I looked down and saw how close her breasts were to my bare arms. They seemed so full and round, so perfect and inviting, that I could only just restrain myself from touching them. I had always assumed that my thoughts of Isabella would remain pure and in the forefront of my mind and was somewhat surprised that, at the first sight of such beautiful women, I should find myself becoming so swiftly overcome by passion. Perhaps I had little resistance to beauty, and fidelity might not be one of my strongest characteristics?

I sought out our friar, and confessed that my thoughts had become lustful and depraved. Although I was pledged to Isabella, it was difficult to love faithfully when I could no longer see the object of my heart's desire.

The friar answered that such ardent yearning for that which we cannot see should be redirected towards the love and promise of eternity offered by our Lord and Saviour, Jesus Christ. I must stand firm and reject the snares of the devil.

This was difficult, because at that moment a group of naked Indian women began to play a game of leapfrog outside our camp.

'You see?' I cried. 'How can anyone avoid the temptation of such flesh?'

'One must not think of these things,' the friar answered firmly, placing his hands together inside his cloak.

'But what can I do to assuage my lustful thoughts?' I asked.

'Think of St Agatha, who lost her breasts for our Lord.'

I suddenly remembered a painting I had seen in Seville of a dark-haired woman holding a tray of pears. *That* was what they were.

'You must have thought about St Agatha a very great deal,' I observed.

'Do not torment me,' the priest replied distractedly, fumbling under his cloak. 'It is a daily agony.'

Perhaps he had a persistent itch, or was cleaning his dagger?

'What must we do?' I asked.

'Look to the Lord,' the friar replied, his voice rising in pitch. 'Only look to the Lord.'

His face was red; his eyes had a faraway look.

Then he gasped.

The man was of no help at all.

I decided to go in search of Pedro for consolation. That was the point of a dog, I had always been told. They offered unquestioning loyalty.

After calling his name several times, I found myself in a small turkey farm. By its side, penned in a small area, were several hairless dogs. Pedro spent a short time snapping and biting at their heels, and then selected a companion for what can only be described as a prolonged act of mating.

All those around me were now involved in acts of lust and bestiality. Was I the only man who had resolved to keep himself pure for his beloved?

After several days we moved on towards the town of Tlaxcala. These people had heard that we were on the march, and it soon became clear that they would not be so easily convinced of our divine status. They had vowed to put our mortality to an immediate test by killing as many of us as possible, their leader Xicotenga informing us that his idea of peace would be to eat our flesh and drink our blood.

We were savagely attacked, and a bloody battle ensued. Pedro was terrified by the noise and I had never seen such slaughter. Our forces only just managed to hold to our formation in the face of some forty thousand warriors. If we had not possessed gunpowder I am sure that we would have been defeated.

Cortés then dispatched messengers to ask for safe passage through their country, and threatened that if they did not agree to this we would be forced to kill all of their people. Exhausted by our bravery, and fearing a further attack, the Tlaxcalans finally surrendered. They bowed their heads, prostrated themselves before Cortés, and begged forgiveness.

That night we attended a great banquet of turkey

and maize cakes, cherries, oranges, mangoes and pineapple, served by the most comely women. After the meal the Tlaxcalans proceeded to display their treasures, some of which would be gifts, some of which we must trade. There were feather mantles, obsidian mirrors, silver medallions, and decorated purses I know Isabella would have treasured; gold saltcellars, gilded beads, wooden scissors, sewing needles, strings, combs, coats, capes and dresses. There were two small alabaster vessels filled with stones that must have been worth two thousand ducats, together with gilded masks, earrings, bracelets, necklaces and pendants.

Yet still I saw nothing that was sufficiently unique to secure my love.

At the end of the ceremonies Chief Xicotenga said to Cortés: 'This is my daughter. She is unmarried and a virgin. You must take her and her friends as your wives. For you are so good and brave that we wish to be your brothers.'

Cortés replied that he was flattered by the gift, but that he would be unable to partake of such hospitality since he was already married and it was not his custom to marry more than one woman.

Then he looked at me.

This was, indeed, a beautiful girl. I realised that the longer we stayed here the harder I would find it to resist such attractions. It was already difficult to recall Isabella's voice, the fall of her hair, the light in her eyes, or the manner in which she walked. It was as if she only existed in her portrait, whereas these women were vibrant and alive, singing into the night sky, building fires, carrying water, and laughing gaily.

It had been so long since I had heard a woman laugh.

Cortés brought the woman over to me. 'Take her,' he ordered.

I could not believe it. These people were so keen to give away their women. Surely this could not be right? How could I remain faithful now?

I looked at Doña Marina.

'Do as he says,' she said.

'But Isabella . . .' I pleaded, 'my betrothed . . .'

'You will be the better prepared to love her . . .' she continued, 'and no one need know.'

The girl led me into a small dark room with a low bed. A fire burned in the corner, and rose petals lay strewn around the floor.

She took off her skirt and lay down on the bed, motioning me to do likewise.

I did not know what to do, but began to remove my doublet. The girl pulled at my breeches and removed my stockings.

Then she placed her naked body against me.

As she pressed her lips to mine, and I could feel her breasts against my skin, my body surged with excitement. She pulled me down towards her. Her nipples hardened into sharp tips, and she began to move underneath me, pulling me inside her. I was unsure what to do, being, I must confess, a virgin, but let her rock me back and forth. I closed my eyes, imagining that she was Isabella, but then opened them again to look at the rise and fall of her breasts. Her eyes widened and she pushed me deep inside her. Within seconds I was brought to the peak of excitement and exploded like cannon shot. It seemed that we could not be more fully conjoined, our sweat and flesh mingling as one body. For a few minutes we lay panting to regain our breath, until the girl pushed me away from her, put on her skirt, and left the room.

It was over.

I was no longer a youth but a man.

Pedro trotted in through the now open doorway. He sniffed at me, rather contemptuously I thought, and then lay down as if to sleep. I began to dress, and made ready to rejoin the men.

When I finally emerged, with a tired Pedro following reluctantly, I saw that my companions had been waiting for me.

Doña Marina came forward.

'That didn't take very long.' She smiled.

It seemed that nothing I did would ever be secret, and that everyone must know my business.

'I'm not sure . . .' I began.

'If she was a virgin? I hope she wasn't . . .' Doña Marina replied.

'I cannot marry her,' I said firmly.

'You are not required to do so. Would you like to see her again?'

'No,' I said, but then thought of her breasts against me. 'How long will we be here?'

16

'Seven nights.'

Doña Marina looked at me, taking my silence as assent.

'I will send her every night.'

I did not know whether guilt or excitement was the stronger of the two emotions flowing through my body, but I knew that I had failed the very first test of my quest.

In the next seven days we began to plan our approach to the magnificent city of Mexico, for we had heard that this was where the greatest treasure lay. The Tlaxcalans urged us against such an undertaking, so outnumbered would we be by the forces of that great city. Even if peace was offered, we were not to believe any of the promises made by its chieftain, Montezuma. But Cortés was adamant, arguing that the whole purpose of our journey was to reach Mexico. He then asked the Tlaxcalans about the best path to the city.

A volcano stood before us, impeding our progress. This was Popocatépetl, and the local people held it in great awe as it rose out of the hills, threatening to spew forth rocks and hot lava over all that surrounded it. We had never seen such a sight and I decided that this was the moment to try my bravery. I offered to climb to the top and report on the best possible route ahead.

Cortés was amused by my boldness, asserting that the loss of my virginity had given me renewed courage, and granted me permission for the ascent. Two chiefs from the nearest settlement of Huexotzinco were to be my companions. They warned that the earth could tremble, and that flames, stones and ash were often flung from the mountain top, killing all in their wake; but I was determined to meet the challenge, whatever the dangers.

It was a difficult ascent and we had to stop at several stages to regain our breath. The light wind seemed to increase the higher we climbed, and the ground was uneven under foot. Pedro picked his way ahead of us, confident despite the sharp stones that lay beneath the snow. At times we had to scramble using our hands across ice and scree, looking down as seldom as we dared. I had never been so far from the level of the sea in my life, and a strange lightness entered my soul, as if I was no longer part of this world. The higher we climbed the smaller things seemed, just as events from our past life recede in the memory and pass into oblivion. Frightened by the unevenness of the ground and the possibility of falling, it seemed at times as if I was dreaming, and I imagined Isabella at the top of the volcano, like the Virgin Mary, dressed in white, judging my infidelity.

As we neared the summit the wind increased, and we could not hear each other speak. But then, looking out into the distance, I saw the gilded city across the plain, shining like a new Jerusalem in the evening light. It was as if I was both in heaven and in hell, and no other land mattered.

The purpose of my journey was clear. Even if I became blind at this moment, I would still have seen the greatest sight on earth. I had done what no man of my country had yet done, and, at the end of my life, when the darkness was closing in, I would be able to say to any man who asked that I, Diego de Godoy, notary to General Cortés, servant of our Emperor Charles, was the first Spaniard to climb the volcano that guarded Mexico. All roads, all settlements, and everything the eye could discern led across the Elysian fields to that noble city. It seemed to float on the water, a cascade of houses, each with its own battlements, each with its own bridge to its neighbour. I had heard people tell of the Italian city of Venice, but this was surely far finer, stretching out in an eternal immensity, lit by a light from highest heaven, beckoning all who saw it to journey across the plain.

I could not see how anyone could ever vanquish such a place, and understood now, in a moment, how all the surrounding peoples could not but submit to its glory.

Hearing of this vision, Cortés became all the more resolved to leave on the morrow, telling the Tlaxcalans that it was God's will that he should continue. It was the eighth of November fifteen hundred and nineteen. Everything we had done on this journey, and perhaps even in our lives, had been leading to this moment.

Four chieftains now approached, carrying a bejewelled palanquin, canopied with vibrant green feathers, decorated with gold, silver and pearls, and topped with a turquoise diadem. The interior was adorned with blue jewels, like sapphires, suggesting the night sky. The figure at the centre stared ahead impassively. Men swept the road before him, and none dared look him in the face.

This was the great Montezuma. He was perhaps some forty years old, olive-skinned and with a slim figure. His hair was dark rather than black, and he wore a well-trimmed beard. His eyes were fine; I could not ascertain their colour, but what surprised me most was the mildness of his demeanour. He seemed gentle, despite his power, as if, perhaps, he never had to raise his voice. Supported on the arms of two chiefs he stepped down and wished our General welcome.

Cortés produced a series of elaborately worked Venetian glass beads, strung on a golden filament and scented with musk. Montezuma bowed to receive them. He then took from his aide a necklace of golden crabs, worked with fabulous intricacy, and hung it on our leader's neck.

'You are welcome to my city, and will stay in my father's house,' he began. 'These men will show you the way, and my people will be happy to receive you. Rest a while and then feast with me this evening.'

He turned away, and his servants carried him off into the distance.

We had never seen such a man, and longed to speak amongst ourselves, but Cortés insisted that we remain silent, warning us to be constantly on the alert, lest we be the victims of some fearsome trap.

That night I wrote my first dispatch.

Sent to His Sacred Majesty, the Emperor, Our Sovereign, by Diego de Godoy, notary to Don Hernán Cortés, Captain General of New Spain.

Most High and Powerful and Catholic Prince, Most Invincible Emperor and Our Sovereign,

The city of Mexico is of some four score thousand houses, and consists of two main islands, Tenochtitlán and Tlatelcolo, linked to the mainland by three raised causeways, each wide enough to allow ten horsemen to ride abreast. It is almost impossible to attack, since there are gaps in the causeways spanned by wooden bridges that can be removed at the approach of an enemy. Many of the people live on the lake in rafts, or on small man-made islands where vegetables grow: peppers, tomatoes, avocado, papaya and granadilla. The lake is filled with people in small boats, catching fish in nets, selling goods or collecting fresh water. Two aqueducts bring fresh water into the city from the spring at Chapultepec, which opens out into reservoirs where men are stationed to fill the buckets of those who come in their canoes.

The city itself has many broad streets of hard earth, and is divided into four areas: The Place Where the Flowers Bloom, The Place of the Gods,

21

The Place of the Herons and The Place of the Mosquitoes. The houses are of one or two floors of stone, capped with flat roofs made either of wooden shingles or of straw laid across horizontal poles. Poorer homes consist of small one-room huts, without chimney or windows, and are made of mud brick on a stone foundation, or of wattle and daub, with thatched gabled roofs. All travel in the city is by bark and canoe, and some of the streets consist entirely of water, so that people can only leave their homes by boat.

The Central Palace has three courtyards, over twenty doors or gates, and a hundred baths and hot houses, all made without nails. The walls are wrought of marble, jasper, and other black stone, with veins of red, like rubies. The roofs are built of timber, cut from cedar, cypress and pine trees; the chambers are painted and hung with cloths of cotton, coney fur, and feathers. Within this palace there live over a thousand gentlewomen, servants and slaves. The soldiers' chambers are hung with a luxurious golden canopy. So beauteous does it seem that even if it were to become a prison, many of us think that we could stay here for all eternity.

On the first night that we stayed in the city there was a tremendous feast. It is impossible to list all the delicacies that were produced: turkeys, pheasants, wild boars, chickens, quails, ducks, pigeons, hares and rabbits. It appeared that anything on earth that moved and could be eaten would be put in front of us. We even heard rumours of human

22

flesh being one of the delicacies, and it would have been impossible to tell if this were the case, so spiced the recipes, so rich the variety of meat. There were locusts with sage, and fish with peppers and tomatoes. There were frogs with green chilli, venison with red chilli, tamales filled with mushrooms, fruit, beans, eggs, snails, tadpoles and salamanders. Small earthenware braziers stood by the side of each dish, and over three hundred men waited upon us, bringing torches made from pine knots when the sky began to darken.

Montezuma sat at a table covered in cloths with Cortés alone by his side. A screen had been erected so that no one should see them eat, and tasters stood at each end, checking the food before it was served. After the meal three richly decorated tubes, or pipes, filled with liquid amber and a herb they called tobacco were placed in front of them. The screen was removed, and Montezuma encouraged our leader to smoke and drink as we watched jesters and acrobats, dwarves and musicians dance and play and sing.

Truly, this is a place of wonders, another world, and I urge Your Sacred Majesty to send a trustful person to make an inquiry and examination of everything that I have said in order that your Kingdoms and Dominions may increase as your Royal Heart so desires.

From the town of Tenochtitlán, dated the fifteenth of November fifteen hundred and nineteen, from Your Sacred Majesty's very humble servant and vassal, who kisses the Very Royal Feet and Hands of Your Highness – Diego de Godoy, notary to Hernán Cortés.

To tell further of the evening would have been to include information only pertaining to myself for which, I am sure, the Emperor had little concern.

Yet I know that it was on this night that my life changed irrevocably.

Five hand-maidens dressed in simple cream tunics now arrived in the banquet bearing an urn. One of these women caught my eye and smiled.

I could not help but stare. Her olive skin seemed to glow in the half-light, and her dark hair shone.

She gestured to the urn, brought over a jug, and poured a deep brown liquid into my goblet.

Bringing the drink to my lips, I found that the beverage had a cool and bittersweet taste, enlivened perhaps with chillies, and that it was not possible to discern its full effect with ease.

The woman nodded at me, encouraging me to continue.

Supping again, the strangely comforting taste began to intrude upon my palate as if one sip could never be enough. It was a liquid that only inspired further drinking, and it began to fill my entire body with its smoothness, as if I need no longer fear the affliction of the world; and all anxiety might pass.

I smiled at the woman and made a gesture to inquire as to the nature of the drink. She replied with one word: '*Cacahuatl.*'

At this the soldiers around me roared, jesting that I had drunk liquid *caca*, and that it would soon emerge from my body as a substance no different from the way in which it had entered.

I turned away with great sadness at their vulgarity. They had not tasted as I had tasted. They had not felt their life change in an instant.

As the meal progressed, I found that I could think of nothing else. I wondered what kind of life this woman led and where she lived. Did she make the beverage, or simply serve it? Perhaps I could learn something of the language and speak to her? The drink had left me so desirous of more that I wondered if perhaps it was a kind of medicine, or if I had been drugged, so tired did I now find myself.

As I lay on my mat that night, under a dais of yellow silk, I realised that I could no longer think of Isabella, but only of the mouth and eyes of the woman who had served me, savouring the sense of ease and peace she had provided. I fell into a deep sleep and dreamed that this woman was coming towards me, slowly and relentlessly, and that I could not escape. Backing away, I could not take my eyes from hers, as she kept walking towards me. Isabella's voice came into my head, telling me to go, to run away, into a forest. I turned and ran, but found myself in an orchard of fig trees, where Isabella's pet canary lay dead on the ground. The lady with the *cacahuatl* was looking down at the bird, and then said, in

Spanish, '*Voló golondrina*', the swallow has gone, the opportunity is lost.

What could this mean?

I awoke with a start, greatly troubled by my dream, and found a return to sleep almost impossible. It was clear that I would find no rest until I saw the lady once more.

The next morning we began our exploration of the marketplace. Stalls filled with exotic and extraordinary goods had been set out as far as the eye could see: embroidered cloths, capes and skirts; agave-fibred sandals, skins of wild beasts, cottons, sisal and ropes; robes made from the skins of pumas and jaguars, otters, jackals, deer, badgers and mountain cats. There were stalls selling the richest of spices: salt and sage, cinnamon, aniseed and black pepper; *mecaxochitl*, vanilla, ground hazelnut and nutmeg; *achiote*, chillies, jasmine and ambergris. Stalls of firewood and charcoal jostled with traders roasting fowl, foxes, partridges, quails, turtle-doves, hares, rabbits, and chickens as large as peacocks. There were even weapons of war, laid out for purchase, as their owners sharpened flints, cut arrows from long strips of wood and hammered out axes of bronze, copper and tin. There were flint knives, two-handed swords, and shields, all ready to be bartered, exchanged or sold.

There were thirty thousand people here, each in search of new delights. The method of buying and selling was to change one ware for another; one gave a hen for a bundle of maize, others offered mantles for salt. But everything was priced, and for money they used the strange brown almonds I had seen one of the natives spill in his canoe when we first arrived. These, we were told, were the beans of the cacao tree, and were held in great regard. One of them could buy a large tomato or sapota; a newly picked avocado was worth three beans, as was a fish, freshly prepared on a stall and wrapped in maize. A small rabbit would sell for thirty beans, a good turkey hen might cost a hundred, and a cock twice that amount.

From another corner of the marketplace rose the smell of cooked food: roasted meat in various sauces, tortillas and savoury tamales, maize cakes, dishes of fish or tripe and toasted gourd seeds sprinkled with salt or honey.

And then I saw the lady who had served me the previous evening, sitting at a stall, carefully grinding cacao beans on a low basalt table. I was lost in amazement, realising that this drink must surely be one of the greatest of delicacies, for she was destroying the actual coinage of the realm in order to create it. If one could only find the source of these beans, and the flower in which they grew, one might perhaps find the secret of all future wealth.

By the lady's side stood a man whom I took to be her father, roasting beans over a fire, sweeping them backwards and forwards with a fan made from rushes. He then sieved them, removed the husks, and poured them onto the lady's table.

Here she crushed the beans with a roller, creating a thick, dark-brown paste which was scraped away into a large gourd and given to a second woman, who now added a little water.

My lady then took the heart of a sapota seed, and began to grind it. This too was added to a small quantity of water, and passed to the second woman.

Then she took some maize, ground it in a gourd and mixed it in the same manner, until the time came to combine all three pastes, which were aerated by vigorous whisking and the slow addition of more water.

And, at last, my lady stood on a chair and poured the finished mixture of cacao, sapota seed and maize down from a great height into a new, larger bowl, where it was whisked into a foaming liquid, and poured into a richly decorated calabash gourd which she held out for me to taste.

I drank of the heady concoction, the foam stretching up towards my nose. It was a strange, almost bitter drink, more spicy in nature than the previous evening. I reached into my knapsack for one of the small sets of bells I had brought with me for barter and the lady smiled so invitingly that I found I could not but meet her gaze.

But then: disaster.

Aguilar, the interpreter, tried to pull me away,

arguing that I was neglecting my duties by indulging in flirtation. He told me that I must rejoin Cortés immediately, and keep a note of the sights we saw.

'What is your name?' I asked the lady as Aguilar attempted to remove me from this prospect of paradise.

She did not understand me, saying again the strange word for the drink she had given me, although this time it sounded different – *chocolatl*.

I pointed to my breast.

'Diego. Diego de Godoy.'

She repeated my words, as if I had two Christian names. 'Diego – Diego de Godoy.'

'Diego,' I insisted, and then stretched out my arm to point to her.

She took my hand in hers and placed it on her breast. 'Quiauhxochitl.'

'It means Rain-Flower.'

The wife of Cortés had appeared by my side.

'You will never be able to pronounce it,' she said dryly. 'Call her Ignacia.'

'After Ignatius of Antioch,' added the priest who accompanied Doña Marina, looking at the girl intently. 'Ignis is Latin for fire, you know. You must burn with love of the Lord . . .'

'And with love for his creation . . .' Doña Marina added tartly, inspecting the girl's body with wry, almost competitive amusement.

Our peace was broken.

'Ignacia,' I said.

'Ignacia.'

She smiled and returned to her work, serving Ortiz, the musician, who began to ingratiate himself immediately. I was convinced that he received the same look that I had accepted myself when first arriving at her stall, and a second violent emotion overcame me, as I moved, in an instant, from incipient passion to total jealousy. I had never known such volatility of heart and felt in such torment that I could have killed Ortiz on the spot.

'Come on,' said Doña Marina, taking my arm. 'We have work to do.'

Lost in thought, I walked through courtyards filled with citrus and jasmine until we arrived before an enormous temple. It was square, and made of stone, raised as high as the reach of an arrow shot from a crossbow. One hundred and fourteen steps stretched up towards two great altars and priests in white robes made their way up and down in ceaseless movement. From the top one could see over the entire city, the lake and the three giant causeways. Although it was one of the most incredible sights we had witnessed thus far, it meant nothing.

I had met Ignacia.

Attempting to write my dispatches that night, I found that no words fell from my pen. I was completely distracted. Whether this was infatuation, desire or love, I knew not; all I did know was that I could not live without seeing that woman again, for what else could account for the sickness in my stomach and the raging in my heart? My only hope lay in Doña Marina. I would have to swallow my pride and confess my love that very night.

'I must see the lady who sells the *chocolatl*. I must discover where she lives,' I declared in as bold a fashion as I could muster.

'Of course we can bring her to you,' she answered abstractedly.

I did not want anything to be done by force.

'No,' I replied. 'I would like to see where she lives.'

'It would not be safe to go there. You would be surrounded by these people, and could be put in danger . . .'

'But they surround us now.'

'What do you mean?'

'You have seen the walls that border our quarters, the causeways, the bridges, and the lake that circles this city. They are like the lattice of a spider's web. We are already trapped and it makes no difference whether I am contained here or with my lady.'

'My lady?' Doña Marina smiled at me, but then stopped for a moment, as if she had not realised the true import of my observation. Lost in thought, she seemed to abandon her concentration.

'I have to see her,' I insisted. 'Will you help me speak with her?'

'Another time.' Still Doña Marina seemed distracted. 'I can summon her, but you cannot visit.

My Lord would forbid such a thing. You are needed here. Talk to me again if you require my help, but do not ask me to disobey our General.'

Later that night I was brought before Cortés. I was fearful of both his company and his temper and was greatly relieved when he received me in all courtesy.

'You have done me great service, Diego.'

'I, my Lord?'

'I too am aware that we are surrounded, cut off even from our Tlaxcalan allies. My chief advisor, Pedro de Alvarado, thinks we should mount a surprise attack and take our chances, but I believe that we should be more cautious. Doña Marina has come to me with good advice, for if you were to be kept with your lady, without fear of harm and in great leisure, how much better and safer it might be if Lord Montezuma were similarly entrapped with us. I have therefore invited him here this night, where he will remain as a voluntary prisoner.'

This seemed an act of unbelievable daring, and I could not imagine how we could explain this to the Mexican people. They would surely rebel. But Cortés continued: 'In honour of our guest I should like you to guard him. I will give you three soldiers, and you must stay with him and occupy his time.'

'What shall I say? I do not have the language.'

'I will give you an interpreter.'

And so, amazingly, it came to pass that over the

next few weeks I was instructed in the Nahuatl language by the great Lord Montezuma.

He was treated in all civility, for we gave the impression that he stayed within our quarters willingly, and that there would be no need for any Mexican to doubt that he was still their ruler. His wives and mistresses were allowed to visit, and he behaved with the utmost courtesy. In the evenings I would instruct him in games of dice, and he would tell of the history of his country so that I could write a full account of this great city.

One evening he even showed me the treasury full of riches gathered by his father. It contained the most extraordinary array of masks, jewellery, urns, bangles and gold. In one corner stood a large vase, which, when I removed the lid, seemed to be filled with the seeds used in the drink Ignacia had given me. I held them in my hand, letting them slip through my fingers.

'Cacao,' explained Montezuma.

I repeated the word.

In this room lay all the fortune any man could ever need. The great chieftain put his arm around me and escorted me from the chamber, as if I was the prisoner and he my gaoler. And, as we sat together and ate that evening, he asked how many wives I possessed.

I told him that I was unmarried, but that a fine and beautiful lady waited at home for my return.

He then asked, now that I had seen his city, if I truly wanted to return to Spain.

I admitted that there was surely no fairer place on earth than this, and that it must seem madness to want to go back home, but I had made a promise, and my word was my bond. I would return to Isabella within two years, having made my fortune, and with a gift no other man could give, a token perhaps even beyond wealth, something as elusive as the Holy Grail or wood from the foot of the Cross of our Saviour.

This intrigued Montezuma, and he told me that he would be glad to provide a brooch, bracelet, necklace or staff that no other man had seen; holy objects, perhaps, from his religion: sacrificial bowls, daggers, statues, or even the smallest and most delicate of objects, a salamander encrusted with lapis.

His generosity and kindness seemed to have no end, and I found it hard to believe that this was the man whose reputation for cruelty and sacrifice stretched out across all these lands and into the approaching seas. I was forced to explain that, although grateful for his kindness, there would surely be many soldiers here who would hope to bring such objects back to Spain.

He then suggested that he should provide me with a small dwelling and a canoe, and that I could return to Spain to bring Isabella to live with me here. We could build a new life in Mexico.

I thought of the way we might live, and could not imagine a world in which Isabella and Ignacia could exist together.

'You are thinking,' he observed, 'that nothing I can give will make you happy.'

I began to speak.

'My great Lord. It is because I am distracted. There is a woman who makes what they call *chocolatl* in your service. If I could see her, the lady who turns your money into drink, then perhaps I could take such things home with me to show my lady.'

At this he laughed.

'This is all that you require? Why not take the lady as your wife? I will give her to you.'

I explained that I did not believe that human beings could be bartered, and that people should only come together freely, not as animals to be exchanged for profit.

'How then will the world survive?' he argued. 'Everything must be ordered. If we all did as we pleased there would be chaos. Even you must have a leader. We must be both leaders and the led.'

'Even in matters of love?'

'I think so,' he insisted. 'It is the best way in which to prevent dispute.'

'Then love is a form of slavery?'

'A slavery in which we willingly enter. What would you have me do?'

'I would like to see the lady who makes the *chocolatl*. I would like to see where she gathers the beans, and how she lives her life.'

'I shall send for her tomorrow,' he answered. 'I

will also show you the secret passage from this palace.'

'A secret passage? Then why have you not escaped?' I asked.

'Because it entertains me to observe your leader, who thinks he has control of me. The more effort he makes in disguising my imprisonment before my people, the more amusing I find you all . . .'

'What will you do?'

'You cannot stay here for ever. I am sure you will tire of us . . .'

I could not understand why so potent a chieftain could appear so kind and weak. It seemed he no longer had any power, and that his wealth was a burden to him. His eyes contained a great sadness, as if all the riches of the world could not bring him happiness, and I realised then that if there were one emotion I would use to describe Montezuma it was that he was bored. He was toying with our presence because it amused him to do so, and he could think of no better jest than to make us think that we had conquered him.

The following day one of Montezuma's servants gestured that Pedro and I should follow him. I was uncertain whether we were travelling north or south or east or west, as we moved through low passageways, strange tunnels, and corridors underneath the temple. It appeared that there was a second, dark underground city in Mexico, filled with stores, supplies, and secret alleys in which people could be hidden away. This place was only known to the court of Montezuma. His tactic had been to concede to each of our wishes, to give us the illusion that we had control of the city and to behave with all courtesy. Then he would either persuade us to retreat, or would have made us so weak and bloated that he could make a strong offensive on our trapped position from below, above, and on every side. All he needed was the right moment to attack.

Emerging from underground, the servant led me through the streets to the edge of the town and left me standing by the side of the lake. He motioned me to wait and immediately departed. I was in a section of the city I had never seen before, and felt certain that I could never return to our quarters without aid.

Pedro's nose twitched with fear, and he looked at me for a reassurance that I knew I could not provide. We were alone with our destiny.

At last I heard the muffled sound of a low canoe, and saw Ignacia, the maker of the *chocolatl*, coming towards us. She pulled in to the side of the lake and motioned me to join her.

I sat behind her as she paddled, the muscles of her back easing back and forth, and wondered what fate now planned for me. I could not help but stare at the way in which her dark hair fell on her bare olive skin. I do not think that I had ever felt such excitement.

Eventually we found ourselves in a shallow

creek, and steered our way through the small islands of the *chinampas*. The air was filled with the sounds of quetzals and toucans. Midges, sawflies, bees and prepona butterflies moved through the stillness of the evening. The trees were lush and shady and so much fruit hung overhead that we did not even have to leave our boat to take figs, cherries, oranges and lemons. Small limestone buildings lay almost hidden in the vegetation and Ignacia pointed ahead to an orchard of low, well-shaded cacao trees growing beneath black-woods and legumes, their large cauliflorous fruits sprouting directly from black trunks. The earth beneath was thick, soft and fertile, as if no one had walked inside these woods before and the leaves of years and of generations had been left to fall and rot, gently nurturing the growth of each new season. My beloved, for that was how I saw her now, steered the boat to the side of the canal, stepped out in one movement, and held out her hand for the rope. I threw it to her. Then she reached back into the boat, removed a silver sickle, and cut one of the large pods from the tree. After splitting it in half, she stretched forward and showed me the brown seeds lying in a soft, white veil, like the caul of a child.

Ignacia then pulled away the white buttery substance, and produced six cacao beans.

'Happie Monie,' she said, in my own language, as if she had learned such words only for me, and gestured that I follow her.

I soon found myself in a series of well-shaded gardens, in which we walked on narrow paths bordered with wild flowers, and past ponds of fresh water used to irrigate the plantation. I tried to think of Isabella but found that I could not; nor did I want to, so excited were my emotions, and so voracious was my desire. Excusing myself with the thought of other soldiers, for whom such activities involved no loss of conscience, I steeled myself with the knowledge that in this country, at least, it seemed common that a man should have more than one beloved.

At last we arrived at a small and private dwelling, hidden in the midst of the plantation. Outside, in a bright space of sunlight, lay wooden trays of cacao beans baking in the sun. Inside, protected against the heat stood a low bed, a table, and storage jars filled with the dried *chocolatl*. There were red glazed pottery jugs, gourds and bowls, and Ignacia now motioned that I should fetch some water while she prepared the *chocolatl*.

I drank from the nearby pond, cooling my neck and forehead, not knowing if it was the heat or my passion which had so raised my temperature.

When I returned, Ignacia held out each ingredient for me to savour before she included them in her mixture, grinding nutmeg, cinnamon and black pepper, adding chillies, aniseed and honey.

She stirred the paste by rolling a carved silver whisk between her palms at speed.

'*Molinillo*,' she said with a smile, as the mixture began to froth.

'He who drinks one cup,' she said in Nahuatl, 'can travel for a whole day without any other refreshment.'

I drank and felt that I need never taste anything else again.

'I need nothing but this.'

'You seem weary. Rest.'

Her voice was as dark and as warm as the *chocolatl*.

Then she gestured to the bed.

Sitting beside me she now took off my cotton quilted jacket and began to rub a kind of butter into my skin, a cream that she took from the pods of the cacao tree. She covered my body, in long sweeping gestures, pressing deep into my flesh, and I knew then that I was lost, that there could be no possible escape from the delights of this seduction, and I gave myself freely to her.

We stayed on the plantation for five days. During this time I drank little but *chocolatl*; it was combined with honey, with flowers, with aniseed, with nutmeg and even with *achiote*, which made the mixture almost red in colour. We always drank from the same gourd. Then we would sleep and play together. All consciousness seemed lost.

At the back of the dwelling was a hot room in which we steamed our bodies, switching them with twigs and bundles of grass, before swimming in the lake and massaging each other dry. We found ourselves half-sleeping, half-waking, in both night and day, and clung to each other as if our bodies could never be separated.

We spoke in a mixed language, part Nahuatl, part Castilian. Ignacia told me that her family had travelled from the far south, from Chiapas, and that they would surely return there. I asked if I would be with her, and she laughed, telling me that we came from different worlds, and could only be together if the earth changed, or if we lived for hundreds of years, or if we lived so many lives, dying and being reborn so often that we would inevitably meet once more, either in this world or the next.

Ignacia spent one whole day making a turkey dish with chillies, vanilla, aniseed and *chocolatl*. She used a small obsidian knife, unfurling onions, slicing the chillies in quick deft movements, and grinding all the ingredients into a thick spicy paste, which she began to beat with the silver *molinillo*. This tool seemed to be the secret to her preparation, as it aired and whisked the mixture at the same time. It was some ten inches long, with protruding spikes, like a miniature weapon.

Water now boiled in pans over fires, the turkey roasted, and as she mixed almonds, raisins and sesame together, she made me inhale each spice before its inclusion in her *mole poblano*. She stripped cinnamon from the bark of a tree and it smelled of early autumn after rain; she broke the petals of star anise, and rubbed my fingers with hers. We ground each spice together and the bouquet of aniseed, cinnamon and almond welled up before us; and then, as Ignacia melted the dark *chocolatl*, the air became heady with the fragrance of onion, chilli and cacao.

I had never savoured such pleasure before. We relished each taste and each minute in which we were together, being gentle both in our conversation and in our love. I had seen how rough soldiers could be, and how brutally they could treat both women and each other, and I had no desire to behave in such a way. As we explored our bodies I wanted to know every part of Ignacia and let her know every part of me. Sometimes I would lie without moving and let her do anything she wanted, stroking and kissing me and bringing me to the point of pleasure before letting me do the same to her. I wanted to give Ignacia the satisfaction that she had given me and she seemed almost insatiable in her desire; so much so, that by the end of the five days we spent together, our supply of cacao butter was quite exhausted.

Pedro, too, had never been happier, chasing rabbits and turkeys, making long forays into the heart of the plantation, emerging on one occasion with a rabbit which he laid at Ignacia's feet, determined, it seemed that she should cook for him as well as myself. It was as if we were a family. Pedro even seemed keen to add to our number, vigorously pursuing yet another Mexican hairless dog and indulging in such a determined act of mating that I began to suspect that his character was rather more competitive than I had first realised.

Yet I must confess that all was not perfection. Ignacia and I could not avoid the difference in our lives and expectations. The conversation began quite innocently, as we lay together in the half-light, when I asked her what she had thought when she had first seen our soldiers. I expected her to say that she could not help but admire the gleam of our silver armour and the majesty of our demeanour.

But for the first time I saw an ineffable sadness in her.

'War,' she said, simply, 'and death.'

'Can we not come in peace?'

'When we have such riches?'

She looked at me as if I knew nothing. 'Pale-coloured men, sons of the sun, the beginning of death.'

I argued, as I had been told but no longer quite believed, that we had come to bring the love of Christ, who had brought us eternal life.

'You have come to destroy our gods and gain great wealth,' she countered quickly.

I tried to explain that the gold here was of the same value as our glass, but Ignacia would not be fooled.

'Do not lie. You want to take our land.'

'That is not the purpose of our travels.'

'Then why have you come?'

I tried to think of all the reasons that were not to do with wealth and conquest.

43

'To find the New World,' I argued.

'But it is not new to us. This is what we have.'

I begged her: 'Do not speak to me like this. I feel great love for you . . .'

'And I for you, but how can this love survive?'

I could not answer her. She kissed me on the lips and moved away, saying only, 'You have a wife?'

'I do not.'

'You have a woman who loves you.'

I could not counter her statement. But I did not know if Isabella had ever truly loved me.

'I hope that you are my beloved.'

'I do not believe you.'

I clasped her shoulders and turned her round, forcing her to look into my eyes. 'At this moment, in this minute, in this hour, and on this day, I love none but you.'

She looked at me in disbelief.

'You know how to use words . . .'

'I speak the truth.'

'I do not think so.'

'Ask me then to prove my love.'

'Renounce your people.'

It came so suddenly, so impossibly.

'You know I cannot do this; it would be the same as asking you to come back with me to Spain, and for you to leave your home and father . . .'

'You cannot do this?'

'No,' I said, 'I cannot.'

I was trapped in Isabella's love; it was an

arrangement from which I could not break free without shame or scandal.

'Then you cannot love me,' Ignacia said simply.

'Trust me,' I said with all my heart. 'I will be true to you.'

'I cannot see how this can be . . .'

'And I cannot see how I can prove it.'

'Swear . . .' she said.

'What shall I swear?'

'That you will never forget me, that you will always love me. Swear.'

'Upon what?'

'Upon this *chocolatl* . . .'

I had never seen her so serious. 'Love me,' she said, taking my hand, as the flames leapt under the pan of melting chocolate.

'I will always love you,' she said. 'And I will always remember this day.'

I repeated her words, and we clasped our hands over the fire.

'Put your hand over the flame, and lift the *chocolatl* away.'

I leaned forward and did so, the heat burning into my hand, pain searing through my body. I was determined to prove that I could do such a thing. Love is the greatest spur to bravery.

'I swear.'

Ignacia smiled briefly and I tried to kiss her, but her movements were now perfunctory. She turned away and lay back on the matting we had so recently consecrated. 'One day,' she said quietly, 'we too will be conquerors. What would you think if we came to your land, and did as you have done to us?'

'I could not be happy.'

'Why not?'

'For you would change the land I love.'

I thought of the glories of Seville, of Isabella and her father, of the town square, and of our fiestas.

'Then why do you think I am unhappy now?' she asked, forlornly. 'Can you not see? You are taking our land.'

'I will try to protect you.'

'Against so many? There is no protection in war.'

She turned away from me, as if intending to sleep, and it seemed there could be no further conversation. I began to stroke her back, but her mind was decided. I knew that she was still awake, but there was nothing I could do or say that would reassure her.

When I awoke, I realised that I had lost all sense of time, and found myself in a state of advanced agitation. I was aware, as perhaps I had never been before, of the responsibilities I possessed: to my General, my fellow soldiers, and myself. I had abandoned my duties, and could think of no explanation for my actions, nor could I write of the things that I had seen and done, so inappropriate were they to a royal report. My only hope of safety lay in Montezuma's reasoning, for he, surely, would provide my alibi to Cortés.

Perhaps he would argue that I had been listing the contents of his treasury.

I told Ignacia that we must leave at once.

She looked at me sadly, and we walked over to our canoe. I could not believe that such a time had come to an end. Ignacia steered the boat towards me and I climbed in with a heavy heart.

As we emerged from the plantation I was filled not only with the impending loss of love but also with trepidation and the fear of punishment.

Ignacia tried to be reassuring as she paddled away from our brief moment of joy, as if she had felt guilty for our last conversation. Perhaps together we could bring peace, she argued. If we encouraged other soldiers to do as we had done, then there was no reason why we could not create a true and lasting settlement and live a life of happiness together.

But I could feel that we were returning to the world of aggression and despair as surely as the tides must ebb and flow. And, as we emerged from the narrow creek of the plantation and sailed once more onto the great lake, we noticed distant fires flaring up on the horizon. The waters were filled with people fleeing the city in low canoes. We could hear the unmistakable sounds of warfare in the distance: orders given, swords striking, women screaming.

'You see,' Ignacia told me, as if she had expected everything. 'Men and violence. It will never end. You love this more than life.'

'It's not true. I am not as other men,' I argued.

'You look at this and tell me it's not true? You have no choice but to be a man. It cannot be otherwise.'

She steered the boat towards the causeway.

'Keep your head low.'

Silently she manoeuvred the boat tight against the side of the causeway so that we were hidden under its lip, lost in its dark shadow. Ignacia tied up and motioned me to follow her through the gate. A whole street had been destroyed and I could see our soldiers fleeing with idols from the temples they had desecrated.

'Go now,' she said, 'back to your people, as I must return to mine.'

Pedro leapt ahead down the street.

'Stop, Pedro, stop,' I called. He waited at the corner, but was impatient for me to join him. It was now dangerous for all three of us, and if we were seen together we could be attacked by any side.

I told Ignacia that I could not live without hope of seeing her again.

'*Quien bien ama tarde olvida.* He who loves well is slow to forget . . .' Ignacia said and kissed me.

'I will always love you,' I said.

'And I you . . .'

Then Ignacia pushed me gently away. I watched in despair as she turned and ran, disappearing down distant streets.

Night was falling. The evening birdsong that I so loved had disappeared beneath the cries of battle. I

48

had no choice but to run through the city in search of the secret passage by which I had come. The Mexican people were raising the drawbridges that linked the houses and streets over the lake, and many had stationed themselves on the rooftops to hurl stones at any Spaniards below. Clinging to the walls of the buildings, and making our path through the shadows, avoiding exposed avenues and keeping under the balconies and parapets, we ran in abrupt and darting movements through the city, until Pedro finally stopped at a wooden door at the back of one of the temples and began to bark. On opening the door we could see the passage by which we had come. The Mexicans were daubing the walls with blood and pulling down the statue of Our Lady that we had placed there.

Pedro and I now plunged back into the dark cavern, illuminated by flares and candles under the faces of gods and demons in our path. The strange underworld was filled with people taking all the weapons, jewels and stored supplies they could lay their hands on, piling provisions into crates as if they too were trying to leave the city. All was panic. I could not imagine anything other than the fact that the Mexicans must be in revolt, and that some calamity must have befallen our leader.

Making my way to the treasury, I discovered that Montezuma's spoils had already been divided – and that our soldiers were in the midst of preparations for a heavily guarded departure. While I had been disporting myself on the plantation, Cortés had been forced to travel back to Vera Cruz in order to defend our mission against an unruly band who had been sent from Cuba to recall our expedition and profit from it themselves. He had left one hundred and fifty men in the capital under the command of Pedro de Alvarado, who had seized the opportunity for the surprise attack he had always advocated, and had turned on the Mexicans as soon as they had tried to free Montezuma.

Surrounded by this chaos, I searched about the treasury. 'The king's fifth' had already been allotted, and was packed in crates ready for our departure. The friar told me that Cortés had claimed one fifth, and that, after double shares for the captains, horsemen and crossbowmen had been allotted, there was virtually nothing left for the common soldier. At this point I must confess that I was filled with a frenzied covetousness, pulling back boxes, peering in chests, casting treasures aside, until at last, in a dark corner, I found the vase with the cacao beans. This I claimed as mine own.

I had discovered the treasure with which I would return and I, alone among my companions, knew its worth. The other soldiers laughed to see me carrying such an object but knew nothing of its contents, and could not imagine the glory it would bring me when I presented it to my betrothed.

I had succeeded in my quest.

Our captains shouted that we should flee, for to

defend our position was hopeless, and our most pressing duty was to remove both ourselves and the treasures that we had secured. Yet when we attempted to make our escape some four thousand Mexican soldiers attacked us.

In the ensuing chaos the city became a place of fear and desperation. It rained heavily, and our horses lost their foothold on the slippery flagstones of the courtyard. Blood and water washed down the streets, and sixteen of our men were killed in the first attack.

In the hell that followed, Montezuma appealed for calm but was stoned to death by his own people. Any attempt at the restoration of order was futile. Cortés returned but had no choice other than retreat. Our horses spurred ahead, fleeing the city, as the Mexicans took to the lake in their canoes, firing at us from all angles, determined that none should live. They broke off sections of the causeway so that we were forced to fight with our bodies chest high in water and could only proceed by holding up our shields, hacking away with the utmost brutality at any who stood in our way. It was a night of blood and rain in which no tactics were effective and the lake slowly filled with the dead, the dying and the terrible remnants of war.

By dawn we had made our way back to the town of Tlaxcala, where we stayed for the next twenty-two days, cauterising our wounds with oil and bandaging them with cotton. We were exhausted, and had no choice but to rest, wash, eat, and recover.

During this time a large section of the gold that we had stored was stolen and the remaining share could not rest in our possession without becoming a source of danger and argument. Cortés took me aside and asked if I would take a group of men back to Spain with the treasure, and put his case for further reinforcements.

I had to follow these orders, and the thought of returning home to Isabella should have filled me with pleasure and relief, but I found that I could think only of Ignacia.

I had to see her again.

The thought of life without her was impossible.

Over the next few nights I began to plan how I might steal away and see her once more. If I was quick, I might be able to return before dawn, without anyone knowing of my departure.

Moving through the creeks and under the trees at nightfall, I knew that any time together would be desperately short, but to part from this land and never see Ignacia again was something I could not tolerate. Pedro checked the route ahead and I crawled through the undergrowth until, at last, we came to the small hut where we had known such happiness.

Ignacia emerged from the doorway, half in sleep and half in fear.

'It is you.'

'I had to see you.'

'You are leaving.'

'I have come to say farewell.'

'This was how it had to be. There is too much gold. Too many soldiers.'

I told her that, although I had to obey my orders, nothing mattered more to me than that I should one day see her again.

'I do not believe you. You will never return.'

'You must believe me.'

'No, no. Only remember me. It is not safe for you to stay.' She turned towards the hut, and fetched a gourd filled with her best criollo cacao beans.

'Take these, and think of me.'

I had nothing to give her in return, no token of my love.

It was as if I no longer knew who I was.

She looked at me sadly.

'A princess was left to guard a secret treasure while her husband was away. Enemy soldiers came. They attacked and tortured her, but she did not say where the treasure lay.'

'This will not happen to you . . .'

'Then the soldiers killed her . . .'

'No.'

'Our people say that the cacao plant grew from her blood in the earth.'

She handed me the gourd in which the beans were held.

'The treasure of the fruit is in the seeds; as bitter as the sufferings of love, as strong as virtue, as red as blood.'

Now she handed me the silver *molinillo*.

'Go safely.'

53

'I will return.'

'The city will be destroyed. There will be nothing left.'

'What will you do?'

'If I have nothing then I will go to Chiapas. If you come back, you may find me there. I know the people.'

I looked into her eyes.

'Wherever you are, I will find you.'

Ignacia took a gold bangle from her arm, and placed it round my wrist. It was as if she was stripping everything away from herself and giving it to me. 'The world is larger than you think.'

'But not large enough for the love we have.'

I had become so well versed in the practice of courtship that now, when I felt more than I had ever felt before, I could not describe my emotions. Everything that I wanted to say seemed as if it came from the *Libro de Buen Amor*.

'You have so many words . . .' she said.

'And all are true. What can I say to make you believe me?'

'That love never tires.'

She looked at me as if she truly believed that she would never see me again. Her voice was filled with the expectation of disappointment, now fulfilled.

'I am no longer myself when I am with you,' I said softly, 'for you have changed me. I am only afraid that something might happen, some terrible disaster which might prevent us seeing each other again, and this I cannot bear . . .'

'You must not be afraid of death. One day you will know that we only come to dream; we only come to sleep. That is one of our songs. It is not true, it is not true that we come to live on earth . . .'

Pedro barked, urging me to return to the boat, and I leaned forward to try and kiss Ignacia once more.

'Wait . . .' She broke off, and turned to fetch a small container from the hut.

'Drink this when you begin your voyage home.'

'What is it?'

'My gift to you. Drink it if you truly think we love each other.'

'Is it *chocolatl*?'

'There are other spices. Drink it as you leave this country, and trust me to do the same.'

'I will drink it now.'

'No. It is better for our luck to drink it when we are apart. If you plan to return it will help you.'

'I will return. I promise.'

'You have sworn?'

'I have sworn.'

'Then let us trust each other. If you are alive then I am alive. Never cease in your search of me.'

We kissed, as if for the last time, as if I might have no other future beyond this moment and my life would be suspended until I saw her again.

'*Quien bien ama tarde olvida.* He who loves truly forgets slowly.'

Ignacia held me to her.

'Say it.'

'*Quien bien ama tarde olvida*,' I repeated.

She rested her hands on my shoulders, and looked into my eyes.

'Love me. Never forget me. Never doubt me.'

'I will always love you.'

'Remember the love we have, however long we are apart.'

We kissed until we could not stand the sorrow any more.

I turned to walk away and then ran, with Pedro ahead, away from the glade to the waiting boat, remembering the first time that Ignacia had brought us here and all the joy that we had shared. I could not bear it. Desperate to escape the gulf between memory and reality, I rowed away from the plantation to join my colleagues, aching with pain and loss, knowing that all my former happiness was past, and that there was no means of avoiding the terrible anguish that now engulfed me.

The next day I was compelled to return to my role as a conquistador. No longer could I live in the world of dream. My responsibilities were clear. I must leave for the coast with sixty men and begin preparations for the return to Spain. Losing oneself in work and duty was, it seemed, the recommended means of forgetting the pains of love, and I set about my tasks like a man possessed, believing that the harder I laboured the more difficult it would be for bitter reality to reach me. At Vera Cruz we worked at a brisk pace, gaining anchors, sails, rigging, cables and tow with such zeal that within a few weeks we were able to set sail for home.

I tried to recall everything that had happened to me, and thought at first of the good fortune that I had enjoyed, my life having been spared by God's grace. But no matter how extraordinary these travels may have been, I could not help but feel that my life would never again be so enthralling. The memory of Ignacia invaded my consciousness. Each night was filled with dreams and memories: the smell of her hair, the taste of the *chocolatl* on her lips, the softness of her skin. One night I dreamed that she was standing in front of the shelter in the glade. She walked towards me and took my hand – as if in search of treasure. We found ourselves behind the dwelling and Ignacia began to dig a hole in the earth with a trowel, bringing out a small wooden box.

She opened it for me to admire and I could see that it was lined with silver and filled with cacao beans. But then she began to walk away, carrying the still open box, and I found that I was unable to follow her. She receded into the distance until I could see that she was standing at the edge of a lake, far away, where she could not hear me and could hardly see me.

Then she tipped the contents of the box into the lake.

Was she pouring our love away? Or was she suggesting that I discard my gift to Isabella?

My dreams were filled with the loss of our love.

Reaching into my knapsack I found the drink that she had given me, full of peppers, *chocolatl* and chillies, and quaffed as if it were the last drink that I might enjoy on earth. It tasted strangely sweet, as if there was some extra ingredient, cardamom perhaps, and I wished that I had asked Ignacia what it was – there was so much that remained unsaid, so much more that we needed to know about each other.

Pedro licked the goblet clean, and we stared out to sea. Looking back now, as I write, I can hardly remember that journey, so numb were my senses, so lost in dreams had I become. At times I took out Isabella's portrait, attempting to look forward to my return, but found that nothing could revive my affection for her. I had become a different man and she must surely be a different woman.

CHAPTER 2

It was a strange homecoming. My father had died and I had little in common with the friends who had remained in the city. Their lives had scarcely changed and they did not seem interested in my travels, preferring to keep the raw experiences of war, death and adventure outside the genteel confines of the court.

On approaching Isabella's house I was filled with an overwhelming depression. I could not see the point of anything in my life, and the love that I tried to recall, however faintly or insincerely, had vanished for ever. I was in the wrong place, at the wrong time, and with the wrong woman.

Isabella was a pale and delicate stranger, as if she had never seen the sun or walked outdoors. She held out her hand and I stooped to kiss its tiny and fragile form, thinking that this must surely be a dream.

'My lady . . .'

'You are much changed,' Isabella ventured.

'I have travelled many miles.'

'And with a beard?'

Her right eyebrow raised itself in amusement and contempt.

'It is the sailor's custom.'

Pedro remained in the doorway, alert, watchful, and unmoved. After two years' absence he no longer knew Isabella. She called to him, but he simply lay down, his head between his paws. Even after she had crossed the room and held him to her, Pedro remained aloof.

'It seems you have corrupted my dog.'

'He has seen much violence, and learned to fear strangers,' I replied wearily. It was as if all my emotions had vanished.

'My poor Pedro.'

'I thought that you had given him to me.'

'He will always be my Pedro.'

An awkward silence followed. After all the perils of separation Isabella and I had nothing to say to each other. Even today, as I write, I cannot understand how endless those two years apart had seemed at the time, and how swift and immediate was the disillusion when we were reunited.

'I long to hear of your endeavours,' she said at last. 'I did believe that you might lose your life.'

'You sound as if you might have wanted this to be so.'

'Only in the most romantic sense.'

We spoke as strangers reciting lines from *The Romance of Durandarte* or as performers in a play in which we had been given the wrong parts. Perhaps she thought me uncouth, for, having seen such suffering, I was no longer the effete young gentleman she had known; and I was saddened, realising that, although I had changed, Isabella had not.

Out of boredom, I reached into my knapsack and pulled out a gold ingot.

Isabella gasped and held out her hand, which then sank under its weight.

'Is this the treasure?'

'It is a present, my love, but the true secret follows . . .'

'And where shall I find it?'

'If you will come to my house . . .'

She sat for a moment and smiled. Her canary sang in the corner, heartlessly beautiful.

'What is that you wear upon your wrist?' she asked accusingly. I had brushed my hair from my eyes, and the bangle Ignacia had given me had fallen forward. For the first time, I felt the need to defend myself.

'It is nothing, my lady, a trifle.'

'It looks like a love token.'

'Believe me, it is no such thing.'

'I think indeed it is.'

'It is merely medicinal. It holds the pain at bay.'

'I have never heard people tell of such a thing. Give it to me.'

'I cannot.'

'You would deny me?'

'I must. It is fixed to my wrist. It cannot be removed.'

'Would you cut your hand off for me?'

'If I did such a thing I would no longer be able to defend you.'

'Would you place it in fire?'

I thought of Ignacia making me pledge my love upon the *chocolatl*, and of how all my words with Isabella were of no consequence compared to that memory.

'I would consign my whole body to the flames if I thought I could win your love . . .' I stated, as boldly as I could, knowing that these rhetorical love games were ridiculous. One could be pledging love and allegiance until Doomsday if one stayed long enough at court. These were amusements of wit, without feeling or passion, and I could not believe that I, who had risked both my life and that of my companions, now lived an existence in which a man's greatest fear might lie in an inadequate reply.

'And, my lady, will you come in search of the treasure I have promised? Will you risk the streets of shame and danger to find me waiting for you?'

I was really quite disgusted with myself.

'The true pleasure lies within my house,' I continued. 'I shall expect you to call upon me.'

'Alone?' she countered.

'Only you must see.'

She would have to visit me unchaperoned.

It was clear that there was little love left between us, and that this conversation had become a game that we both wanted to win. But although unnerved by the threat to her dignity, Isabella pretended that it mattered not that we should be alone when she made her visit. She would brave the possibility of scandal and take her part in an encounter for which we had waited for two long years.

'I will come as night falls and stay for a single hour. You will escort me home after I have seen my treasure?' she conceded.

'You may depend upon me.'

'Then I will leave you to make ready for my arrival.'

I now had the rest of the day to prepare for Isabella's first taste of *chocolatl* and I headed straight for the marketplace. Walking through stalls selling rugs and furs, trinkets and jewels, melons and oranges, I could not help but think of Ignacia. Many of the spices we had prepared together in the glade could not be found, but with good honey and vanilla I thought it might at least be possible to make a similar drink to the one she had prepared for me. I would use her best criollo beans, keeping the vase from Montezuma's court safe for further use should the recipe be a success.

Returning to my lodgings in the Barrio Santa Cruz, I dismissed both maid and cook, determined that I should be alone with Isabella.

Pedro would be our chaperone.

Taking the best beans from the store Ignacia had given me, I began to prepare the paste, mixing the ground cacao with water and stirring the mixture vigorously with my *molinillo*.

I realised that this was my first attempt at cooking unaided.

The thought at first amused me, and then put me into a state of dread, for it soon became clear that all was not proceeding as it might have done. I had been too hasty in dismissing the cook, and found that I was somewhat hapless in the kitchen. The paste before me had the bitterest of tastes and refused to froth; the mixture would not smooth; and even after I had added both vanilla and honey, my creation looked completely unpalatable.

At this moment Isabella arrived, far earlier than I had anticipated.

This was not at all satisfactory.

'What are you doing?' she asked.

I confess that I was flustered.

'This,' I said, pointing at the mixture before me, 'is the food of the gods.'

'And what, pray, is it called?'

I looked back down at the paste.

'Caca . . . caca . . . caca . . .' My senses had clearly left me.

She looked at the brown mixture as if she had never been so insulted.

'It is a glue?'

'No. It is a most unusual drink.'

'You expect me to partake of it?'

'It is not finished. It is not perfected.'

'And this is the treasure of which no man yet knows?'

'It is.' I smiled hopefully.

Isabella looked at me in disbelief.

I did not know whether to laugh or cry, for this was either the most terrible confrontation or the perfect opportunity to escape a match I dreaded.

'It is a type of drink – the word *atl* is the Mexican for water . . .' I explained nervously, looking at the flames of my fire, 'and *choco*, yes, *choco* means bitter. It is a kind of bitter water. Choco-atl – chocolate.'

Isabella looked at me as if I was a madman.

I began to froth the mixture, and picked out a small spoonful.

'Try,' I offered, before realising that I had failed to taste it myself.

Isabella leaned before me and drank.

An expression of sheer revulsion swept across her face.

'It needs some improvement. I do not have all the ingredients,' I apologised on seeing the contortion of her facial features.

'I cannot believe that you have done this . . .' Her expression seemed little short of utter hatred.

'It is a very great treasure,' I added simply.

'You have insulted me,' she said.

'No, Isabella, I have not.'

She took a deep breath, and then unleashed her venom.

'I am glad I came alone, because I could not have borne this humiliation to be witnessed by anyone. I have kept true to you, refusing the offers of Bernaldino Heredia and Francisco de la Cueva, both from good families, and both handsome men, only to find that you have returned with an insult greater than that borne by any other woman in the city: a concoction baser than the excrement of your dog.'

She turned for the doorway, brushing past a surprised Pedro.

'It is a good drink. It simply needs refinement. Let me see you once more,' I asked, desperately.

'From now on, you will only visit me in company, at which I will offer only the customary courtesies. Do not fear; I will not slight you. I am a lady. But I will never forget or forgive you this day, and you can no longer expect any favour from me.'

I was so nervous that I wanted to laugh.

'Do you think this is funny?'

'No.' But the situation was so terrible that I was, indeed, filled with a desperate merriment.

'Do you?'

'This is the gift of which no man knows. I have fulfilled my quest.' I smiled.

'There can be no greater insult. Think only of how you can redeem yourself, and pray to the Lord in Highest Heaven that he might, after a prolonged period of penance and self-mortification, forgive you this most grievous of sins.'

And then she was gone.

For the next few weeks, together with María and Esperanza, my maid and my cook, I seldom left the house. Pride filled my being and I became obsessed with the desire to make my chocolate recipe a success.

During this period of seclusion I began to learn the art of preparing food to perfection, until I was able, under the watchful eye of Esperanza, to make a few of the finest delicacies a Spaniard could hope to enjoy: tamales, tortillas and menudo; empanada de bacalao, seviche de camarones, and pollo al pibil. Spices arrived in the marketplace from the Orient, from the Indies and from Africa, and I even endeavoured to recreate the Mexican sauce, the *mole poblano*, that Ignacia had cooked for me, filling a turkey with chocolate, chillies, spices, raisins and almonds, in preparation for a future banquet. Furthermore, by proper addition of vanilla, sugar and spices in good measure, the yolk of an egg, and with an impressively insouciant action with the *molinillo*, I was also able to make what seemed to be the perfect chocolate drink.

Esperanza then invited Sylvana, Isabella's own cook, to share a meal in our company. This large and humourless woman was initially suspicious, and I feared that she might complicate matters by telling her mistress of my plans, but as the chocolate began to beguile her palate, her face broke out into the broadest of smiles, as if she was a child who had been given the key to a secret treasure chest.

'Even if I never taste such delights again, I know that I can die a happy woman,' she declared. 'Tell me everything you know about this wonderful ingredient. It will change our lives for ever.'

The two women resolved that Isabella should be given a second chance to appreciate the finer points of chocolate. Together, and with my help, they would make a *mole poblano* for the Feast of St James, a day which was to be celebrated by a banquet at the house of Isabella's duenna.

Here at last was the chance to restore my dignity.

Nights passed in relentless anticipation. I was determined to prove that I had fulfilled my quest, and that I was a true adventurer, worthy of the respect of those who had done little with their lives apart from staying in Seville.

I was a conquistador.

Isabella would not humiliate me.

When the day finally arrived, the kitchens sang out with activity, María and Esperanza joining with Sylvana to create a feast for eighty people while I sought out extra provisions from the markets. Almonds, chillies, olive oil, vanilla, aniseed, raisins, sesame were now combined with the last of the criollo beans that I had received from Ignacia. It would be a feast for the gods.

As well as supervising the creation of the meal in secret, I was to be one of the guests, Isabella's father remaining ignorant of the turbulence of our relationship. However, when the time came to take our seats at the table, I discovered that I was placed as far as possible from my former love. A slight was clearly intended for I found myself situated between two elderly crones of indeterminate age, both of whom appeared to be profoundly deaf.

Isabella sat like a princess, coldly beautiful in a green silk dress, her eyes half hidden behind a golden fan, dividing her attentions between a bibulous and somewhat swarthy soldier, and a pale young man who looked as if he might have played the lute.

This made me all the more determined upon my revenge.

The banquet had been announced as a celebration of the bounty from the New World, and the guests were treated to a selection of the delicacies I had first tasted in Mexico: watermelons, guinea fowl, partridge, quails and maize cakes; cherries, prickly pears, pineapples and mangoes. The diners were bemused by the rich array on offer, talking of each dish in turn, relieved that there should be some subject on which they could speak to strangers, yet unwilling to reveal their true opinions in this polite and withheld society. I listened to my deaf companions pronounce upon the achievements of their children and the possibilities they had spurned in earlier parts of their lives: loves, dowries, travel and ambition – all thwarted – until the turkey finally arrived upon the table.

Here at last was the food which I had prepared, its sauce as rich and as dark as molasses.

I watched Isabella take her first taste of the meat.

She seemed to avoid the sauce, pushing the turkey gently away with the tines of her fork. I fixed all my concentration upon her, as if she should eat by the sheer force of my will; and, as she eventually placed the turkey and the *mole* in her mouth, her face contorted into the strangest of expressions, moving from tentative fear, through momentary disgust, to an aftertaste of unbounded pleasure.

The room was hushed at last. Every guest was beguiled by the taste of the sauce – at first smooth and reassuring, then fiery, and at last explosive in the mouth, softened by the sweet flavour of the turkey beneath. It was, one man pronounced, the original ambrosia, a dish so alluring that all delicacies he had previously enjoyed were dismissibly ordinary. The guests fell to, unable to speak, concentrating only upon their food, as if the sauce was nothing less than the lost elixir of silence and delight.

Minutes passed, and still it seemed that Isabella's guests could do nothing but relish the chocolate which now coated their tongues, bidding them on to speechless joy.

At last, and still silent, the guests reached for wine and water, fearful indeed that such familiar flavours might corrupt their palates. The speed of eating slowed, as if they wished to conserve and revere every mouthful. The room was filled with pleasure. Perhaps Isabella had some dim memory of the taste, for she sat as if reminded of a dream.

At last she gestured to a servant, and whispered in his ear.

He mouthed the word '*Mole*'. When Isabella asked to be told of the ingredients, I fixed my gaze upon her, and waited to lip-read from the servant the word '*Chocolatl*'.

Instantly she looked up and her eyes found mine in a fury.

She threw down her napkin, but the swarthy man next to her stayed her hand, as if all who attended this banquet had mysteriously been given the gift of gentleness and courtesy. The pale lutenist murmured in surprise, unable to believe that there could be anything not to her liking.

Isabella paused, lost in thought for a moment, and returned to the meal.

I had won my victory. All that could be heard in the banquet hall were contented sighs until, one by one, the guests finished eating.

Isabella's father then called for Sylvana, the cook.

As she entered the room, the guests at the banquet burst into spontaneous applause.

'We will have this meal, exactly as we have enjoyed it, on the same day, every year, for the rest of our lives,' called Isabella's father.

'Every year? Every week!' shouted Gonzalo de Sandoval, amidst much laughter.

Sylvana looked slowly round the assembled gathering of appreciative faces, blushed, and then burst into tears, as if they had been mocking her.

I rose from the table and followed her into the kitchen, where she sat, head in hands, inconsolable.

'How can I make such a feast again? Where will we find the ingredients?' she cried.

I reassured her that we still possessed the vase of beans that I had taken from Montezuma's treasury and that all might yet be well. We simply needed time and patience in order to work out a plan.

Unfortunately, as is so often the case, neither Sylvana nor I were in control of our destiny. For the very next day Isabella arrived at my home, alone, and unannounced.

She wasted no time in coming to her point.

'It was you.'

'I do not know of which you speak.'

'Why did you do that?'

'What?'

'You know perfectly well. Do not dissemble.'

'Very well,' I answered as calmly as I could. 'I did this simply to show you that I could do such a thing. To prove worthy of your love.'

'You bribed the cook.'

'I did no such thing.'

'You gave her the means and taught her the art of making it.'

Now I relished her fury.

'I did.'

'And it is the talk of the Barrio Santa Cruz. None can forget it; everyone longs to taste such food again. You have power over me, for we have no means of reproducing such a feast without appealing to your generosity.'

'The meal cannot be made without cacao beans, I do confess.'

'Then give me some.'

'I only have a small supply remaining.'

'Show me.'

'Very well. But if you accept the gift, then you must accept my love.'

Of course I did not want such a love, particularly now that I had it within my grasp. I sought victory, forgiveness, dignity and, perhaps, it must be confessed, although I am ashamed to admit to such a thing, Isabella's humiliation.

'Show me.'

I pulled out the vase that I had carried from Montezuma's treasury.

'These are cacao beans,' I said, 'more precious than gold, for when you drink the chocolate concocted from them you are drinking your fortune.'

'This is the true treasure?'

'They must be kept dark, and hidden well.'

Isabella was hardly able to contain her impatience.

'Give them to me.'

'This vase has been sealed,' I continued, speaking as if I were a conjuror, 'and none has touched it but myself. You will be the first – and last – to see these beans since they were placed in Montezuma's treasury.'

I pulled off the seal.

Isabella's eyes glistened.

'Can I touch them?' she said.

'Of course,' I replied. 'Take thirty beans away with you tonight. Sylvana knows what to do.'

She stared as if they were holy relics or the wafers for Mass. 'Surely this is a great treasure that makes men fall so silent at its taste.' I had never seen her so moved.

'Is this truly my gift?' she asked.

Victory.

I had met the conditions of her challenge.

'Take the beans. My felicitations, my admiration, and my deepest respect for your beauty go with them.'

'I have mistreated you, Diego.'

'No matter,' I said, solemnly.

'You have my love.'

If Isabella had said such a thing two years ago I would have fallen into a swoon.

Now it meant nothing.

Yet I stopped for a moment, knowing that a life of ease and grace awaited me if only I chose to take it.

Such are the attractions of wealth.

'Come to me tomorrow,' Isabella continued. 'I will take these to my cook, and we will taste this elixir once more.'

She held out her hand for me to kiss.

'Farewell. My father will wish to see you to discuss the marriage dowry. You have succeeded in your quest.'

And with these words she returned to court.

María and Esperanza were delighted by my victory, and began to plan for their immediate employment in the ducal household.

What had I done?

Fear filled my heart as we approached Isabella's house the next day. My servants wore their finest clothes, and had instructed me to trim my beard and wear my sword. This was to be the beginning of my new life at court.

The thought gave me no pleasure. Was I to be trapped within the expectations of civilised life? How could I ever return to Mexico? Life was now a dream in which I was carried further and further away from Ignacia. What was I doing?

We walked up to the gatehouse of the Quintallina residence, and knocked boldly on the door.

Imagine our surprise therefore, when the gate-keeper then directed us to the servants' entrance.

Here Sylvana was waiting for us.

'Impostors!' she cried. 'Deceivers! Adulterers! Crooks!'

She picked up the vase that I had given Isabella, raised it above her head, and, with a great heave, threw it onto the ground, smashing it in pieces before us.

Cacao beans rolled onto the courtyard.

María and Esperanza shrieked at the waste, but Sylvana only shouted all the more.

'Criminals!'

Pedro raced forward and began to sniff at the

cacao beans. I knelt down beside him and was immediately surprised by their softer texture.

They felt like crumbling cork.

I tried to break a bean in my hands, but it would not yield. Perhaps they were stale?

I raised it to my mouth and bit gently.

There was a strong taste of dried clay.

The beans were false.

They must have lain undisturbed in Montezuma's treasury because they had been confiscated as counterfeit money. That was why such little attention was paid when I picked up the vase. People knew them to be fake.

I had been made a laughing stock.

I felt a surge of heat well up in my face, knowing that I must seem either foolish or malevolent.

From Sylvana's words I came to understand that her mistress had thought that I had played the cruellest of tricks upon her. I was never to be allowed near her again.

My life in Seville was at an end.

I returned home to think about my future.

Without fortune, chocolate or a betrothed, I now had the freedom and the excuse to risk my life upon the seas and return to Mexico. If Ignacia was alive and still loved me, then I would fulfil my promise to her, and even find happiness. If not, then I would have nothing.

But it was clear that I must venture all upon that love. It was the only hope that might give my life purpose and meaning.

CHAPTER 3

N othing can convey my despair when my eyes first caught sight of the black and charred remains of that great city of Mexico, its towers destroyed, its people either dead or destitute. The vast marketplace lay empty. The majesty of the city had passed away. Houses were left derelict and the temples had been laid waste, their treasures drowned in the lake so that none should profit from them. It was as if Pedro and I had entered an abandoned world. No one we passed seemed able to tell us what had happened or where we might find survivors. This was a city of ghosts.

We found a canoe and paddled through the *chinampas*, past tree after burned-out tree. All that had previously been good and fertile had been destroyed. We travelled as if in a nightmare, unable to find respite from the succession of sights that awaited us. Approaching the former shelter where I had last seen Ignacia, despair entered the very soul of my being, a dread and a fear of death that I think has never left me to this day. I expected the worst, despised myself for expecting such a thing, and was both terrified and filled with self-hatred when my fears were confirmed. For there, in the distance, lay the burned remains of the adobe dwelling where Ignacia and I had found such happiness only two years before.

With mounting terror I scoured the blackened vegetation until I found a small mound.

My heart emptied.

Could this be Ignacia's grave?

Pedro whimpered and began to paw at the earth.

If I was to know what had happened I would have to dig away at the mound, uncovering what lay inside it, even if it meant the discovery of my beloved's body.

I was terrified by the dangers of such knowledge, but knew that my life could not continue if I did not know what had happened. I found some sticks and began to dig, as if Ignacia had been buried alive and we only needed to pull the earth away to let her breathe once more.

'My God, let her live,' I prayed.

Pulling away soil, leaf, plantain, and cacao husks with increasing urgency, we finally revealed the edge of a white tunic beneath the earth.

Overcome with the most sudden and appalling grief, I could not bear to dig any further and began to re-cover the mound with earth, as if I had never begun the idea of exhumation, desperately trying to hide the memory of the discovery; as if my initial curiosity had never happened, and none of this was happening to me. Utterly disorientated, my head filled with pain and confusion, I wanted to run away, to be any place save here, but found that I could not move. Everything about my life had been suspended.

I knelt at the grave, with Pedro by my side, and wept.

My people had done this.

My people had killed the woman I loved.

It seemed that everything I had sought in life, all that I believed in no longer possessed any meaning. And the more I reflected on my helplessness before a history that I could not change, the more furious I became, losing my faith in justice, a divine creator, and the power of man to shape any kind of destiny.

As dusk turned into night, Pedro and I lay down on the ground and slept like sentinels by Ignacia's grave. We would stay here in quiet bereavement until we were able to recover. Even though our mouths were dry and our stomachs empty, I could neither eat, nor drink.

I could not imagine being anywhere else on earth.

The next morning I covered the mound with jacaranda blossom, praying for the reincarnation of Ignacia's soul.

At least we would try to honour her memory.

We stood over the grave for many hours. Perhaps the night came, and the sun rose, but I had no sensation of day or night, life or death, energy or exhaustion. I was sick with emptiness, unable to move until it became clear that our lives could not continue in this way, that we must try to endure bereavement, even if it meant an existence with no real respite from sorrow.

I laid a pile of stones around Ignacia's grave, and carved her words to me around the bark of a tree: '*Quien bien ama tarde olvida*. He who loves truly, forgets slowly.'

And then Pedro and I turned away from the plantation as we had done so many months before, slowly and reluctantly, our footsteps pointless and uneven, stumbling blindly away from the place that had seen both the greatest happiness and now the greatest misery of our small lives.

We returned to Tlaxcala. There I sought out people who had been in the Mexican campaign and asked if they knew of any who had survived the siege of the city and the battle for its possession so that they might tell us the story of what had happened.

The *cacique* told me that he had seen groups from the city heading south, as far as Chiapas, to seek allies, whether old or new, to build up their broken lives. After a series of meals and conversations I told the man of the reason for my travels, and of my love for Ignacia.

As my speech became increasingly desperate with grief, I wondered if the more I talked the greater might be the possibility of Ignacia being alive after all, as if, by talking of her, I could force her back into being; that she could live, tangibly, once more, because my memory of her was so strong. Perhaps the grave might not be hers, perhaps I could find her again, perhaps she lived after all?

I think that I was hysterical with sadness.

The chieftain took pity on me, expressing deep sympathy at my loss, and offered another wife in Ignacia's place.

I informed him that I only wanted Ignacia. I could love none but her.

The *cacique* seemed almost amused by my loyalty and looked at Pedro.

'One man, one woman, one dog.'

'It is all that I require for happiness,' I replied.

'You want happiness?' he asked incredulously.

'I do not expect it. I simply seek it.'

There seemed little choice but to cast our fate to the winds and head for Ignacia's home of Chiapas. Perhaps her surviving relatives might tell us what had occurred. Perhaps they would allow us to live in the love and memory of her.

Outside the city, the land seemed as vast as the sea, and Pedro and I found ourselves lost between plain and mountain, sun and moon, noon and midnight. We must have seemed such small figures, adrift in the grandeur of an infinite and hostile landscape. The fierce rays of the sun were almost unbearable, our thirst seemed unquenchable, and each day I had to make bandages for Pedro's feet so that the searing heat of the sand would not burn his paws.

We built fires at night, cooking simple meals where we could, and huddled together against the cold climate and our fear of the future. We slept in the open under the stars. The heat from the fire made me dream of flames, of travelling down an endless series of corridors in a great palace, all opening out into vast landscapes, but all on fire, impenetrable, a labyrinth of avenues in which Ignacia appeared in the distance, endlessly unreachable.

Pedro and I suffered days of fear and nights of loneliness, not knowing if we lived or dreamed, forever dependent on the kindness of strangers.

It was an eternity of travel.

I could hardly count the days or measure the years that we walked through pine-forested hills, past the stone sentinels of the Atlantes of Tula, following the course of lakes and waterfalls and crossing dry sierra until we climbed up the mountains and reached, at last, Ignacia's home of Chiapas.

Approaching a man drinking from a water fountain, I asked in the native tongue where lodgings might be found. After admiring Pedro, he took us to a solid brick house in a narrow street and introduced me to a woman named Doña Tita. She lived in a house occupied entirely by women who, I soon guessed, sold their favours for money (and from my soldiering days, I remembered a woman once taking one hundred cacao beans for her pleasure).

Doña Tita proved to be a lady of both sensuality and wisdom. She also had a great affection for dogs. Taking pity on my plight, and recognising me to be an educated man, she informed me that I could stay in her lodgings without charge if I was prepared to teach her son the rudiments of Latin and let her walk Pedro each evening. This I gladly agreed, and although her son was a somewhat obstinate child of eight, I could see that there might be benefits in staying in such a place while I searched for some sign of Ignacia's family.

That night I asked the ladies of the house if any people had arrived in the last year from the city of Mexico, for I had known a girl of great beauty there called either Ignacia or Quiauhxochitl. Perhaps I did not express myself clearly, but Doña Tita and the ladies of the establishment seemed confused by my questioning. They told me that they knew none by that name, although so many people arrived from different places, it was impossible to know everyone.

I then informed the assembled company that if she, or any of her relatives, had arrived here it would have been after the siege of Mexico.

At this the ladies stopped and stared at one another.

'This was long ago,' said Doña Tita.

'No, no,' I replied, 'I was there but two years ago.'

At this the women began to laugh and shake their heads.

'You are strange. Perhaps you are ill after your travels. There is no one called Ignacia or Quiauhxochitl here . . .'

I did indeed feel faint.

Had I travelled all these days and nights to be disappointed?

That night Doña Tita came to my room, and asked if I needed any further comforts. The girls in her care had been amused by my arrival and wished to hear a full account of my adventures. Perhaps I would be good enough to take chocolate with them?

I told them that I would be glad to help in the preparation. This would be my chance to win their trust, and we soon fell into conversation about the best ways in which to drink chocolate. The ladies were extremely interested in my opinions, and were impressed by my insistence that they should add vanilla before the drink was whisked. They also admired my silver *molinillo*, believing it be an object of some antiquity, but I hastened to assure them that it had newly come from Montezuma's court, as I had been there at the time of the siege.

Again, the women seemed amused by my response.

'Sir, we have heard of this war from our grand-fathers. If you truly witnessed the fall of Mexico, and are not merely a teller of tales, then you would have to be over a hundred years old.'

'I was there, I tell you.'

'It cannot be,' said a dark and fiercely attractive woman known as Doña María.

'No, truly, I was there. I was beloved of a woman whom I called Ignacia. I saw the great Montezuma.'

'Love has touched his brains,' another observed.

'More chocolate,' said Doña María, quickly, as if she wished to cease the conversation.

It seemed that they were dismissing me as a man who dissembled and could talk no sense. I felt dizzy with fear. Was this another of my dreams?

Doña Tita saw my distress.

'Rest,' she said, gently, 'rest, sleep and dream. You will be better in the morning.'

I closed my eyes and began to drift away. Perhaps when I awoke all would return to normal.

The ladies now turned their attentions to Pedro, stroking his ears through their fingers, rubbing his stomach, and playing with him in a manner of which I did not altogether approve. But it seemed as if this too was a dream, an erotic fantasy. Not knowing if I was awake or if I dreamed, I turned away to sleep well and long, leaving any attempt at understanding until the morrow.

At daybreak I took Pedro for a walk around Chiapas. It was a crisp autumn morning. Churches, missions, homes and a small government assembly began to reveal themselves as the light slowly brightened. In the main square I saw a fantastically decorated cathedral with vine-draped columns and vegetable motifs as if it had been enforested in stone. It could have been Santiago or Cadiz, so majestic was its presence, and I could not understand how this building could have been constructed so recently and with such speed. People now emerged from their houses and began to fill the streets, and Pedro raced ahead to greet them. Yet on closer inspection, the townspeople were dressed in a manner that I had not seen before, and seemed to move at a far faster pace than I considered normal.

What was happening to me?

It seemed as if we had stumbled into another New World. Spanish women wore tight bodices and elaborate farthingales in which it must have been extremely difficult to proceed, while the men dressed in effeminate cloaks, unbuttoned doublets and ribboned breeches in which it cannot have been possible to perform any real labour. Chamula Indians were clothed in long white woollen tunics rather than tasselled loincloths; Zincantecans wore pink costumes with ribbons, while their women were dressed in blue rebozos, gathered white blouses, and black skirts wrapped around their hips. In these garments they set out to work in Spanish plantations full of tobacco and cotton under the hot sun. The Indian slaves worked from sunrise to sunet, and there was little of the joy in their faces that I had seen in the Mexico that I remembered. The town had become a factory, and

I felt hardness in my heart when I saw the way in which we Spanish had assumed power and lived a life of indolence and disdain, never venturing into the fields where those good people toiled for so many hours.

I soon became disorientated and returned to my lodgings fearing the onset of the debilitating faintness that threatened to overpower me. Back within the comforts of my room, I found myself falling into a deep sleep in which I dreamed once again that Ignacia was for ever unreachable.

I awoke to find Doña Tita mopping my brow. She listened patiently when I eventually told her the story of my life, but then explained, as if to a child, that if my story was true, I must be over one hundred and forty years old. I should understand how hard it was for the women with whom I now lived to believe me.

Thinking of all the events of my former life I acknowledged that some strange fate must have befallen me. Time seemed to have slipped.

Doña Tita encouraged me to spend as much of my recreational time as possible in quiet reflection. She would care for Pedro while I undertook a long convalescence. How long I spent in this fashion I know not, but I do not think that I had ever experienced such loving concern. Two of the girls in the hostelry, Doña María and Doña Julia, even offered me the pleasures of their bedroom, their dark-red blouses revealing much of their breasts beneath, but although sorely tempted, I was too confused to accept their kind proposition, fearing that my brain, already touched by fever, might be tipped into madness by the delights of their flesh.

But as soon as I had regained a modicum of strength, I asked if I could attempt to return to normality by helping the ladies to prepare their meals.

I believed this would not only provide me with unchallenging labour which might aid the restoration of my sanity, but could also give me time in which to think on my past, reconstruct my memory, and plan my future life.

The women accepted my offer with much amusement, doubting my abilities in the kitchen, but asking most particularly for the chocolate recipe of which I had spoken.

'We know what you can do with your *molinillo*,' they laughed.

And so it was that my composure slowly returned. The ladies helped me to crush sugar cane and cinnamon, added to sweeten the paste. We also included orange blossom water, almonds and dark ambergris before experimenting with different quantities of aniseed, vanilla, chillies and hazelnuts. The hostelry became a veritable laboratory of chocolate and I think our most exceptional breakthrough came when we decided that such a drink might be better prepared by adding hot water at an earlier stage of its creation. By mixing two teaspoons of boiling water into the first mixture of powdered cacao, vanilla and cinnamon, we were able to make a thicker and smoother paste. The heat of the water helped the cacao to melt and then, by adding the mixture to a beaten egg in the bottom of a serving jug, we created such a dense and richly textured creation that it was almost possible for a ladle to stand within it.

The first time we tasted it we knew that we had invented an utterly transcendent concoction.

The women gave the drink to their customers, and the men even took the recipe home to their wives. It became a sensation in the town and word spread that I had created a veritable nectar.

Every time I made it I could not help but think of Ignacia. The chocolate became my means of remembering her, the warmth of the aroma never failing to take me back to the happiness we had known on the plantation. I was filled with the recollection of the completeness we had shared, mourning its passing, and lived within the dream of that memory, away from the cares and troubles of the world.

After a few months people began to tell me that they were quite unable to live, even for a few hours, without the ingestion of my hot chocolate, and that they would surely die if they were denied it. Indeed they confessed that they had been made mad by their passion for it.

The women even let it be known that they were now unable to endure the length and solemnity of Mass in the cathedral without resort to this refreshment. Their small round bellies ached for chocolate and they would perish if denied it for more than an hour. This consequently occasioned the arrival of their maids in the middle of the Divine Service, bringing hot chocolate to aid their mistresses so that they might bear the contemplation of temptation, sin and the mortification of the flesh with equanimity.

This ingestion of chocolate by so many of the women in church inevitably caused great interruption. The congregation could hear neither Epistle nor Gospel, so great was the clatter of consumption and conversation. After a few weeks the Bishop of the city opined that this insatiable activity, and the opportunity to exchange glances, looks, and even conversation between friends, appeared to be the veritable climax of the Divine Service, and that the women were replacing the sober ingestion of the body and blood of our Lord and Saviour with an altogether more worldly refreshment. He denounced the drink from his pulpit, warning that if this interruption of the Mass did not cease then he would be forced to ban the taking of chocolate altogether.

The women were horrified, and gathered together in resistance. Such a ban could not be countenanced. They could not live without chocolate.

Their first recourse was to seduction.

After a great amount of discussion, Doña Tita dispatched herself to the house of the Bishop and pleaded with him for lenience, eventually offering

90

the comforts of her bed if only he would allow her to take chocolate during the Mass.

This was a brave and dangerous strategy, risking further condemnation, but the Bishop wavered in the midst of his first test, drinking Doña Tita's chocolate and contemplating her delights. It was clear that his chastity and sobriety might not survive for long, since Doña Tita was possessed of the most extraordinary beauty, and if the Bishop had ever wondered about the temptations of the flesh, he could tell that he would surely learn of their delights more speedily from this extraordinary woman than from any other living mortal. Only by a lifetime of self-discipline, repression and restraint did he manage to steady himself against her charms, and he asked her to leave without granting her any concession.

But Doña Tita knew that the man was tempted, and was pleased when the Bishop sent a gift the next morning to thank her for her visit, offering her an open invitation to his house and enclosing a necklace of orange and black rosary beads, consisting of the vividly hued peas of the fruit known as *abrus precatorius*. This he urged her to wear directly against her ample bosom as a talisman to protect her from evil.

Doña Tita delighted in the gift, and wore it through many a hot afternoon of her labour; but once the Bishop discovered that she still enjoyed the ardour of men in ways denied to him, and had refused to alter her behaviour at Mass, he returned to his attack on the drinking of chocolate with renewed vigour. He issued a proclamation, excommunicating any that saw fit to eat or drink within his church.

The women of the city, far from being chastised by this fierce instruction, became positively militant, and sent messages to the Bishop stating that they could no longer continue to attend Mass under this new ordinance, for they would die of pain if they were forced to do so. They took to their houses, refusing to leave for even the smallest of trifles, sending messages to each other by their maids, and denied their husbands the favours of the marriage bed.

The Bishop stood in his ornate baroque pulpit and preached to an empty cathedral. Quite unmoved, he made it clear that he preferred the honour of God above that of his own life.

This remark was to prove fatal.

For it was well known that the Bishop still took chocolate in his own home. His page, a young man named Salazár, had been ordered to stir the drink each evening while repeating the words of the *Salve Regina*. His Grace believed that this was the only manner in which chocolate could be whisked to perfection, for it would then reach a perfect level of froth on the final *Amen*.

Unfortunately, Salazár was not as faithful to the Bishop as might be expected, for he spent many nights in the arms of Doña María, the sister of Doña Tita. She had informed him of my new additions to the chocolate that they drank, and how its taste had improved quite immeasurably. She felt certain that the Bishop would enjoy the new configuration of his favourite bedtime beverage.

Salazár then returned with the ingredients for my recipe, telling the Bishop of the delights awaiting him if he did but try the drink, if only as a means of understanding why the women of the city were so distracted.

At first his master was suspicious. He was also angered by the time Salazár took in its preparation and the delay before he could hear the reassuring sound of his familiar prayer.

Salve, regina, mater misericordiae
Vita, dulcedo et spes nostra, salve!

When the page returned, the Bishop took one sip and adamantly refused the concoction.

'This chocolate does not taste of the *Salve Regina*.'

Salazár removed the drink and stirred again, reciting the prayer once more. He could not understand how the Bishop, a positive misogynist, should so desire the invocation of a prayer by women, about women, and for women.

Ad te clamamus exsules filii Evae,
Ad te suspiramus gementes et flentes
In hac lacrimarum valle.

He returned, the Bishop tasted again, but still no satisfaction came.

'This is not how I like my chocolate.'

For the third time Salazár removed himself to the adjoining room.

Et Iesum, benedictum fructum ventris tui,
Nobis post hoc exsilium ostende,
O clemens, o pia,
O dulcis virgo Maria.

At last he returned.

The Bishop took up the drink, his face clouded by doubt and weariness. But then, as he drank again, a strange sense of calm possessed him.

'That is better,' he replied, 'most sweet.' He sipped again. 'It fills the mouth, leaving no other need.'

It was to be his last drink upon this earth. For Doña María had included among the cardamom, cinnamon and chillies, a well-ground mixture of jimson weed, henbane and belladonna.

After ten minutes the Bishop clasped his stomach and fell to the floor.

In the next few hours he became increasingly feverish, crying out that he had seen visions of the Virgin made in chocolate, of Jesus nailed to a chocolate cross, and of the disciples eating his flesh and blood. He shouted Doña Tita's name in passion and vengeance, and fell into a wild delirium. Physicians were sent for, but their aid was futile. The vitriolic priest was dying of the deadliest of poisons and the chocolate had disguised its taste to perfection.

The Bishop took a week to die, his body swelling to such an extent that the slightest touch caused his skin to erupt. His blackened fingers fell away from his hands, and thick white liquid seeped from his skin. The physician pronounced epithelial necrosis and oedema of rumen, reticulum, and liver.

This, then, was death by chocolate.

The dispute was over. The women dutifully donned their robes of mourning but were inwardly delighted that they had won such a victory. They would corrupt a new priest, and the drinking of chocolate would continue, uninterrupted by the demands of the Mass. Life could return to normal.

But three days after the death of the Bishop, a curious event befell us. At daybreak on the Sabbath, Doña Tita fell ill and died herself.

This was strange, for she had always been the most vigorous and lively of women, and we were at a loss to understand what could possibly have caused her untimely demise. There was no contagious illness in the town and no other woman had suffered from such a fever. Only after the physician had searched her quarters most extensively was the cause of her death discovered.

The rosary given to her by the Bishop had proved to exude a deadly poison. It had seeped into Doña Tita's body through her skin during the sweat of her amorous labours. The more energetic her lustful endeavours had become, the more swiftly the poison had entered her body, until after several days and nights of love she had been so ravaged by the essence of *abrus precatorius* that she gave up the ghost.

Clearly this was an extremely dangerous town in which to live, and I began to fear for my own safety: a suspicion that proved justified later that night when I awoke to find Pedro barking furiously and Doña María lying full across my chest, straddling my body with her fine legs.

Her hands were placed firmly around my neck.

'Give me the recipe,' she hissed.

'What recipe?' I asked, my waking consciousness now filled with sweat, fear and, even, I was horrified to realise, desire.

'You know very well.'

Her dark hair fell forward, and she pinioned my arms with her knees. Although Doña María was, I could see, magnificently and defiantly desirable, I could not ignore the fact that she was attempting to strangle me.

'Let me go,' I gasped.

'Only if you give me the recipe.'

'I have.' I could speak so little that every word had to count. 'You know full well how the chocolate is prepared. That is what has led to all this trouble.'

'Not the chocolate, you fool. You know what I want. My father has died. My mother has died.

Seven of my sisters have died. I am now in mortal danger. I must possess the secret of the true elixir. Give it to me.'

'I do not know what you mean,' I answered in all truthfulness, but again she tightened her grip.

'I have kept silent all this while, but now that such trouble has befallen us all, I will not let you go unless you tell me the secret. You must have drunk the true elixir. And your dog too,' she added peremptorily as she kicked Pedro away from me.

It was then that I realised what she was talking about.

Perhaps because I was slow in the way I lived my life I must also be slow in thought. It had taken me all this time to understand what had happened.

Ignacia's drink.

She had given me a liquid that could slow, or even halt, the process of ageing.

'Well?'

I rocked my head to indicate that I could not speak, and at last Doña María lessened her grip. I gasped violently. What could I do? Even if I told no more than the truth, I knew that this woman, a vile poisoner whose advances I had spurned when I first came to the town, would never believe me.

'A friend gave it to me long ago,' I answered at last, my voice full of fear. 'I do not know the recipe.'

Doña María pulled out a knife and held it at my throat. It was clear that I would either have to summon up a last reserve of strength, or deceive the woman by creating a false elixir and then run from the city with all possible speed.

'Don't lie to me,' she hissed. 'Our fathers perfected the art of slowing the pace of life. You know that you could live for a thousand years.'

'What?'

'I said a thousand years. Now tell me the recipe . . .'

'I do not have it.'

'Tell me, you bastard.'

At this point, and I do not know now why Providence should have aided me in such a fashion, the soldiers of the town arrived at the door below, and banged at it furiously, demanding that they speak with me immediately.

Four men strode manfully into the room. I turned my head as far as I could and saw that they had stopped in astonishment. Apologising for their interruption, thinking that Doña María and I were at the point of climax in a strange sexual love-game of lust and depravity, the soldiers told me that I was to be expelled from the town. Because I was well known for my chocolate sorcery, I must be, in part, responsible for the death of the Bishop.

Not knowing which was the greater of the dangers in which I found myself, I informed the soldiers that the tragic incidents in the town were not of my making, and that I had scarcely even met the Bishop.

But the soldiers were adamant, pulling Doña María away from me, and hauling me before them.

It was clear that since I had brought the recipe for death by chocolate into the town, I must now leave with it forthwith.

'Take it,' one cried, 'take your vile drink away from this place so that we might never see it again.'

Another told me that although his wife had promised him that one sip of my chocolate would change his life and cure his boils, he had felt nothing. I was, according to him, nothing more than a quack, a false apothecary, a mountebank.

I explained that I had never made any great claims for my recipe, and had only been trying to bring a little pleasure into the world, but the soldiers were adamant.

I was to leave the city immediately.

They escorted both Pedro and myself to the town gate, and told me never to return, even if I lived to be a hundred years old.

Resisting the temptation to make a sardonic reply, I decided that silence, and an extremely speedy escape, would surely be the best course of action.

My life had been spared.

But what were we to do? My head was filled with unanswered questions. Had Ignacia really provided us with the elixir of life? Or was this simply a drug that made our lives far slower than those of any other mortal? Why had she not partaken of the drink herself? And how or why had she died, leaving me with Pedro to travel in solitude, without love, across the lonely desert of the future?

We had been cast into an endless drift across the chaos of history. And if we were to live far longer than any person we might meet, with no one to share our fate, then we were surely destined to a life of loss and disappointment, constantly bidding farewell to all those we loved, unable to share the rhythm of their lives.

Was this to be a living death?

And then I wondered if the drink was not so much an elixir as a kind of sleeping draught, and that I was immersed in a dream from which I could not wake. How could I tell that everything that had happened to me had truly occurred?

Filled with such confusion, and uncertain as to where to go or what to do, we at last made our way to the coast and boarded *La Princesa*, a two-decker Spanish galleon that would take us back to Seville.

Perhaps if I returned home, life might revert to normal.

Once on board Pedro and I spent much of our time below decks in contemplation of our fate.

Around us, the Atlantic raged.

In the eye of a fierce storm, I clung to the sides of my bunk, as if its confined wooden space was already my coffin. Pedro tried to sleep by my side, but was too frightened by the unpredictability of the raging seas around us, and fell, like me, into something of a fever. Unclear whether it was night or day, and troubled again by confusion as to whether I lived or merely dreamed, my brain teemed with anxiety. I thought of Ignacia again, running through the fiery corridors of a labyrinth, unable to escape, impossible to rescue. The heat intensified through my dream, and the air was pierced by strange cries and distant gunfire. Then, as Ignacia disappeared down a long avenue of flames, my bed shuddered violently, and tilted desperately to starboard under the weight of a terrible blast of explosive fire.

We were under attack.

Taking Pedro under my arm, I raced onto the fore-deck to see a French ship of some hundred and ten guns approaching us under fighting sail. The gale in which we found ourselves made both ships plunge heavily, but the French had begun by attacking our masts and rigging so that we were unable to manoeuvre. It was almost impossible to defend ourselves as the ship listed in the gale. Water began to flood the lower deck through the open gun ports, and it was clear that we might capsize at any moment. Our fore and main masts were carried away. Lines jerked and fell loose, yards hung in the slings, and canvas flew. All I could see before me was a chaos of canvas, cordage and broken spars. The air was alive with the crack of battle and the despairing cries of men engaged in a valiant struggle to conquer and survive.

Our crew were desperate to keep their gunpowder

dry but, at half past three in the afternoon, the arms chest blew up in our faces and set light to the quarterdeck. Fire raced towards us, and men frantically poured water onto the raging flames. The lower parts of our heeled decks were awash, the gun crews wading waist deep in water as the ship rose and fell with the waves, a doomed wreck of flood and fire.

The French now turned to attack the body of *La Princesa* rather than its rigging, bombarding us with fierce broadsides. Whole pieces of plank flew off the ship and the French, having gained the higher water, rained so much fire down upon us that our starboard side was pierced like a colander. The captain and some nine other sailors were killed, and although the fighting continued until darkness fell, it was clear that we could not possibly survive this great blaze and wash of battle.

The storm and conflict subsided with the oncoming night but our ship was a shattered wreck. Dismasted and disheartened, we had no choice but to surrender. As a pale grey dawn broke slowly across the sky, a boarding party arrived from the enemy, not so much to claim our ship as to rescue survivors.

The French captain informed us that this was *'fortune de guerre'*. We were his prisoners, and we were to return with him to France by the powers invested in him by his King Louis XVI.

I was taken aboard their ship, with Pedro

clinging to me for dear life. The French sailors laughed at us uproariously, pointing at my fashionable garments with great mirth, jeering at our humiliation.

Fear struck at my heart.

On inquiring as to the year of the Lord in which we now found ourselves, I was informed, to my great amazement, that it was seventeen hundred and eighty-eight.

I stopped as if in a stupor. I could not believe that both Pedro and I had slipped out of time once more. How could we be nearly three hundred years old?

Perhaps this, too, was a dream from which I could not wake? Or perhaps I was persistently involved in one dream, with other dreams within it, like a succession of wooden dolls, each tightly encased, one within another? For there seemed to be no escape from the nightmare that was my existence, no anchor to steady the ship of my being, and the memories of my former life seemed as fragile as the fragments of our wrecked galleon.

The winter journey across the Atlantic was long and arduous, and did nothing to aid my sanity.

On arrival at the frozen port of Honfleur I was taken to Paris. The sailors who held me captive did not know what to do with me, arguing amongst themselves that they would never achieve a good price, for who would want to take, even as a prisoner or slave, such a deranged Spaniard and such an unappealing dog?

I could do nothing to convince them otherwise and, indeed, it often seemed that the more I tried to explain myself the worse the resulting situation became. There was certainly no persuading them that I was sane, and I only regretted that they could not change their mind about Pedro who had proved himself to be the most noble, the most reliable, and the most loving of companions.

At last it was resolved that until clear orders were received from the Admiralty there was little choice but to keep me in an institution until my fate was decided.

And that is how I found myself in the Bastille.

CHAPTER 4

Eight round towers, some seventy feet high, with walls as much as five feet thick, now loomed above me. The portcullis was raised and guards searched me from head to foot. I was made to change into an ill-fitting pair of trousers, a long shirt and a large hooded dressing gown with a ludicrous cap. Although I knew for certain that I was not insane, I certainly looked so now.

The Governor, Bernard-René de Launay, a kindly man, allowed me to keep Pedro in my cell, and entered both our names into the Bastille register. A small, red-faced turnkey called Lossinote then led us to a room high in the Corner Tower.

The prison was, in truth, a dark and terrifying dungeon, filled with all manner of weapons of destruction. Climbing the narrow stairway, we passed a vast armoury in which were stored some two hundred and fifty barrels of powder. Pikes and axes hung on the walls and the prison reeked of dankness and disease. Each step we took through the gloomy building made me realise how impossible it must be to escape, and how crazed the prisoners must be.

My cell was octagonal in structure, perhaps twenty feet wide, and rose to a vaulted and plastered ceiling. A high triple-barrelled window was the single source of light. The only furniture was a folding table, three cane chairs held together by a few remaining strings, and two aged mattresses.

'How long will we be here?' I asked.

'No one ever knows the answer to that question,' Lossinote replied mysteriously.

My bed was crawling with mites, my shirt itched with lice, and the gruel they provided for my evening repast was inedible. Pedro lay exhausted on the cold floor, and we fell into further despair.

It was several months before I discovered that each prisoner was entitled to a weekly allowance and could make certain requests. After placing Pedro's needs first, acquiring a blanket, grooming comb, and dog bowl, I asked for a decent supply of clothes: twelve shirts, ten handkerchiefs, two coats, a double-breasted waistcoat, tight satin breeches, silk stockings, shoes, and even, at last, a peruke, which I hoped might make me seem more French.

Unfortunately, this was not a success and I decided it would be better to keep my hair long and dark in the Spanish style to which I was accustomed. But I was determined that I would no longer look like a clown, and shaved off my beard, taking pains with my appearance (there was so little else to do), and keeping myself and my dog as clean and as well groomed as we could possibly be.

It then occurred to me that the linen that had been supplied could be put to good use, and I began to unpick sections of my shirts, sheets and blankets, thread by thread, in order to construct a home-made ladder with which we might plan our escape. I thanked God that I had spent so much time on ropes, ratlines, lanyards and dead-eyes during my first sea voyage, and I remembered, with fondness and regret, my friends and colleagues from those times: Cortés and Doña Marina, Montezuma and, of course, my beloved Ignacia. It seemed so long ago, but I knew that without memory I could have no real existence. These events had defined my life, and I must not forget them if I was to retain my sanity.

And yet, as I threaded and wove my way towards what I hoped would be my freedom, it was impossible not to feel inexpressibly lonely. I was cut off from my past, and uncertain of my future. My days were enlivened only by the perambulations in which I was allowed to exercise Pedro and by the opportunity to share meals, once a week, with any fellow inmate whom, it was felt, would benefit by my company.

It soon became apparent that none of the prisoners had actually committed any serious crime. There was a man who had been arrested for forging lottery tickets, and another who had been taken for a madman after he had tried to bottle clouds; there was a third with a feverish voice who claimed that he knew the location of a secret treasure but had refused to tell where it was; and there was a priest who had done nothing more than impregnate the daughter of a count. The only man I spoke to frequently was the oldest person I had ever seen, a Major Whyte. Nobody knew how long he had been in the prison. He could not remember himself and was even more detached from his past than I was myself, believing that he was Julius Caesar. The whiteness of his hair and the length of his beard amazed me. If this indeed was extreme old age, a mixture of infirmity, delusion and amnesia, then perhaps I was fortunate in delaying its arrival for so long.

Yet there was also another person in the Bastille, a gentleman, who kept himself both solitary and aloof. I would see him between the hours of noon and one, a mysterious figure with sombre gait, walking on the ramparts, silhouetted against the sky. He was overweight and elderly, perhaps five feet and six inches tall, with a high forehead and an aquiline nose. His hair was powdered and coiffed, and he was dressed in a blue overcoat with a red collar and silver buttons. He was closely followed by a man whom I was later informed was his servant, Mérigot; employed, I was told, because the elderly gentleman had now grown so fat that he was unable to change even his shirt without assistance.

My gaolers told me that I should be advised to avoid all conversation since the gentleman was almost as mad as I was myself. Such a warning did not, however, concern me, since it was clear that if we were not mad when we entered this prison, we were certainly made so inside it, and that if I avoided lunacy altogether there would be no one to speak to at all. At times the gentleman looked up in my direction, as if I might be a distant friend or relative that he was attempting to recognise, but then turned his attention away, seeming to gaze far beyond me, into the distance, as if he had been touched by some great thought.

This made me all the more determined to speak with him, and I ventured to create an opportunity by which our paths might cross. Only after some three months could this be achieved when we met on a narrow stretch of the ramparts, unable to pass each other without at least some small exchange of words.

'Sir,' said the corpulent figure, stopping before me. 'I admire your greyhound.'

'He is my sole companion,' I replied.

'Although I prefer a setter or a spaniel myself.'

'He was given to me a long time ago.'

'He has a lean head and a spirited eye. What is his name?'

'Pedro.'

The man began to circle round us, and my greyhound followed his movements with suspicion.

'He has a strong well-coupled back, muscular thighs and a deep brisket. There is good length from hip to hock, and his feet look tight. His tail is like the lash of a hunting crop. He must cover good ground . . .'

'He does.'

'And I imagine he has plenty of stamina.'

No one had admired Pedro with such an appraising eye before, and I was pleased that this fine gentleman was taking such an interest in him.

'You are Spanish,' observed the man.

'I am . . .'

'Yet you speak excellent French . . .'

'I have, it seems, a talent for languages.'

'I have always maintained that the best way to learn a foreign language is to have an affair with a woman twice your age.'

I was startled by the boldness of his observation, but he spoke as if every phrase could not be doubted and as if each statement was an order to be obeyed.

'You must visit me in my chambers.'

'You are allowed visitors?'

'I have guests among the inmates, and I am allowed certain foods. My wife brings me pâtés, hams and fruit preserves. I cannot abide the vomit that they provide here. Messengers come with almond paste, jellied quince and kumquats, cakes, spices and soaps. I want for nothing but company and freedom.'

'I thought this was a prison,' I observed, failing to understand how this most sombre of institutions could be the pit of hell for so many of its inhabitants and yet a visiting hotel for others.

'It is.'

'And you can eat whatever you choose?'

'Whatever my wife brings me. There is only one thing I lack.'

'And what is that?'

'Chocolate. I have a most particular desire; and yet it is denied me as a punishment.'

'On what grounds?'

'Recalcitrance. Are you permitted such a thing?'

'I do not know what I am allowed. I am told nothing.'

'Then you must tell them. A man should not be made to suffer without understanding why. This is not the Spanish Inquisition.'

'Indeed not.'

He eyed me beadily, but I kept my counsel, saying: 'The guards have told me that these are difficult times for food of quality. There have been riots over bread . . .'

'The people in the streets are restless. They shout for bread, yet it lies piled in Saint-Lazare. There is plenty if you know where to seek it. I have excellent connections, and can assure you, Monsieur, that the times are not so difficult as to deny us chocolate. Perhaps you could ask for some in my place.'

'I will try to do so.'

'You know about chocolate?'

'I do, my Lord.'

I hesitated.

No.

It was too ridiculous to begin my story.

'And what is your favourite method of taking chocolate?'

'It is as a drink, combining chocolate, cinnamon and vanilla.'

'Vanilla?' He smiled secretively. 'I am very fond of vanilla. It can be put to excellent use. Yet have you not tasted a violet chocolate cream, a chocolate mixed with the petals of roses, or even a pastille?'

'I have not . . .'

'Then how can you have lived?'

'I have spent many years travelling . . .'

'And what have you done for money?'

'I have taught Latin. I have worked as a notary and as a scribe. And I have even cooked . . .'

'A cook?' He stopped, suddenly excited. 'Then you must come to my rooms as soon as possible. We will make chocolate together. Ask the gaolers to go to Monsieur Debauve in Rue des Saints-Pères; he is the purveyor of chocolate to the King.'

'They think I am insane.'

'But no more insane than the other inhabitants. Come with your dog, and come with chocolate. What is your daily allowance?'

'Nine *livres*.'

'That is ample. Monsieur Debauve has an excellent breakfast chocolate. He also sells a chocolate flavoured with salep for the fortification of muscle, an anti-spasmodic chocolate with orange blossom, and an almond-milk chocolate for the irritable. We shall need them all.' The man was suddenly both animated and beneficent, as if the prospect of chocolate had sealed our friendship. 'I will order the remaining ingredients: cream, syrup, raspberries and, of course, cognac. We shall have a feast, and tell each other the story of our lives; what, pray, is your name and title?'

I paused, but because he thought me to be already mad, such caution was no longer necessary.

'I am Diego de Godoy, a notary for General Hernán Cortés, servant of the Emperor Charles V.'

The man in the overcoat made a low bow, as if trained in an age of manners now long past. On rising, he looked me in the eye, and said in a low voice, 'And I am Donatien Alphonse François, Marquis de Sade.'

I returned to my room in a state of exhilaration; here at last was a man of distinction with whom I could converse. How much of life is improved by hope, by the introduction of new friendship, and by new possibilities. I was almost happy.

How long was it since I had last been content?

How quickly the mind can move from joy to despair. As if from nowhere, the memory of Ignacia entered my soul once more. I could not stop thinking about her, but now doubted not only my memory but also my feelings. Perhaps I had begun to idolise her, just as I had worshipped Isabella. How could I test such emotion?

And what indeed was love? Had I really known it, or was it just a mirage, like everything else in my life? Would I ever understand that which was real, and that which was not? How could I trust anything?

All these questions needed answers, and I began to believe that the Marquis might be able to provide them.

I resolved to bring him chocolate as soon as I was able.

His room was fine indeed, and so opulent was the furniture that I could not believe that we were still in prison. Four family portraits hung on the walls; tapestries, decorated velvet cushions, and cotton fabrics were thrown about the chamber; and soft, clean, quilted mattresses lay in two corners. An open *nécessaire* revealed a lavish assortment of clothes: velvet coats, satin breeches, silk stockings; tricornes, broad-brimmed beaver hats and damask nightgowns; buckled shoes, jack boots, spatterdashes and Hessians. A roquelaure cloak and a surtout were strewn on the chaise longue. Books lay scattered on every surface, and the room was lit by a plentiful supply of candles. The Marquis had even perfumed the air with orange flower water.

'My humble dwelling . . .' He smiled.

Food was laid out all around us; there were

fresh marigolds in a vase (he informed me that he received flowers every week) and a bowl of raspberries lay on an antique bureau.

'You have brought the chocolate?' he asked.

'I have.'

'Then let us drink some first. Mérigot' – he snapped his fingers – 'prepare the *chocolatière*.'

I looked across the room and noticed a white porcelain jug decorated with blue flowers, handled, and lidded, with a stirring spoon. The Marquis followed my observation and added, 'I had the *chocolatière* made for me. It is very fine,' before moving towards the fireplace.

A bowl of water was boiling in preparation.

'Let us begin,' he cried. 'We shall make raspberry liqueur creams, I think.' He placed the chocolate I had brought in a bowl suspended over boiling water, and the rising steam soon began to melt the chocolate.

'Stir this slowly,' he ordered, handing me a spoon. 'Mérigot, the moulds.'

The servant crossed the room with a silver tray of some thirty hollows, which he held in his left hand. Taking my melted chocolate in his right, Mérigot then poured the mixture into the moulded tray, returning the remaining chocolate to the heat when he had done so.

'I would never have thought that I should one day be making raspberry crèmes in the Bastille,' observed the Marquis gleefully.

In one brisk movement Mérigot then inverted his

115

tray, pouring the remaining chocolate back into my bowl. The chocolate clung to the scooped hollows, lining the mould.

'Behold,' sang the Marquis, 'the very roofs and domes of our crèmes. Let them harden in the cool of the window ledge. It is a good crisp day and the indigo clouds that so often beset us have not yet formed – never make chocolate when the atmosphere is moist, my Spaniard, never let water touch it lest the mixture seize.'

I stopped for a moment, amazed that this cell, once a prison and then a salon, had now become a kitchen.

'Keep stirring the remaining chocolate, my fair Spaniard. Concentrate.'

As I resumed my task I wondered why the Marquis was in this place at all and asked him if he had committed any crime.

'It was nothing. Mere libertinage. I have a mother-in-law who is the *fons et origo* of all viciousness.'

'What did you do?'

'It was nothing.'

'Nothing?'

'They say that I poisoned some prostitutes and seduced my wife's sister.'

'And did you?'

He was amazed by my impertinence: as if I should have dared to ask such a question.

'Of course I did no such thing. The prostitutes came willingly; my sister-in-law loved me.'

'And your wife?'

'She understands.'

'It surprises me that you should say so.'

'It has always interested me, the things that people will do for a title.'

'But the lady herself . . .'

'In thrall to her mother. And, of course, to me. This chocolate needs a stronger stir.'

'I have the very thing . . .' I said, reaching into my knapsack.

The eyes of the Marquis now burned with curiosity in the midst of his somewhat bloated face.

'And what, pray, is that?'

'My *molinillo*, Monsieur. It comes from ancient Mexico.'

'Give it to me.'

He picked up the instrument and began to feel its length.

'This is a most excellent object . . .' He was clearly in great awe.

'I know of no better means of stirring chocolate,' I said.

'Indeed,' he replied, testing the *molinillo* by whisking a bowl of cream, sugar and raspberry brandy over a low heat.

'I like to whip up a good cream,' he observed distractedly, before returning to his recipe.

'Now, Spaniard,' he cried, looking at me, 'you see that bowl of raspberries? They have been soaking in brandy these past few days. Place one raspberry in each of the moulds. I will fill them with this cream. We will allow them to harden while we have our soup. Then we must cover the bases with the remains of our melted chocolate, and scoop them out at the end of our feast. It will be perfection.'

I began to dot the raspberries in the moulds as Mérigot prepared a funnel. The Marquis removed his cream from the heat, and continued to stir the mixture.

'My crème is at its peak,' he cried to his lackey. 'You have the necessary tool?'

The servant held the funnel, and the Marquis scooped the mixture into the bag.

'Diego de Godoy,' he ordered, 'bring me the platter if you please.'

I brought over the tray, now lined with chocolate and filled with raspberries. Mérigot then squeezed the cream into each of the chocolate moulds, filling them to the brim.

'Very good, Mérigot. Excellent,' commended the Marquis. 'Now we can rest before completing the bases.'

Imperiously, he brushed his servant aside. 'Clear, Mérigot, clear. The Spaniard and I must drink our chocolate.'

Two china cups and saucers had been laid on the table before us and the Marquis picked up the *chocolatière* and began to pour out the chocolate.

'These are *trembleuses*,' the Marquis informed

me. 'They too have been specially made for chocolate.'

He settled back in his chair.

I drank the wonderfully viscous, bittersweet mixture. It was so rich that I did not know if I could eat a full meal after I had partaken of it. Its velvet texture was as the smoothest cream.

'It settles us for a life of leisure, does it not?' the Marquis opined. 'Nothing can provide a greater sense of well being.'

'It soothes the palate and stimulates the heart,' I replied.

'Richelieu's brother uses it to bind his bowels, you know,' confided my companion.

Mérigot now cleared the cooking into what appeared to be a side chamber as the Marquis and I sat drinking chocolate and talking of our past. Although he evidently thought my life a fiction, I related its course as factually as I could, and he was amused by many of my adventures, taking particular interest in the sexual proclivities of the women in Chiapas.

'What a paradise that must have been,' he concluded, 'a paradise. Such a pity you had to leave.'

'I was glad to do so.'

'With so much still to explore? Shame on you, my fair Spaniard, shame on you.'

The meal arrived. It was the most sumptuous repast I had experienced since the dinner given in Isabella's house so many years before. Mérigot was the perfect showman, displaying each dish in turn:

sorrel soup, artichoke terrine, and an almond and monkfish mousse, followed by partridges stuffed with Muscat grapes, red mullet sausages in chervil butter, medallions of foie gras, roast chicken with pine kernels, a gasconnade de pintades, cuttlefish cooked in pastis, marinated artichokes, stuffed courgette flowers in a tomato coulis, goat's cheese truffles in olive pâté, Cressane pears, a nut galette, fresh grapes, four bottles of old burgundy, the best mocha coffee, and a large bottle of Armagnac.

It could have fed the entire prison for a week.

There was even a separate tray for Pedro, containing beef, mutton, horseflesh and maize, raw fruits, milk, beans, and boiled fish. He looked at me with a mixture of mistrust and amazement, as if we had rediscovered the New World once more. I think that we were both filled with good humour, so warmed and comforted were we by the hospitality of this fine gourmand.

In the middle of our repast, the Marquis summoned Mérigot once more.

'Have you completed the backs of the chocolate crèmes?'

'I have, my Lord.'

'Then bring them to me.'

'I fear they are still warm. They are not ready to be turned out.'

'Bring us samples. Two to savour.'

'Very well.'

'I like my chocolate as black as possible . . .' The Marquis gulped at his wine. We were now onto our third bottle. 'As black as the devil's arse.'

It was odd to hear him speak so crudely and I must confess that it puzzled me, for he was a man of the most exquisite manners.

The chocolate now arrived, together with two glasses of ice-cold water. Mérigot advised that we cleansed our palates so that we would be ready to discern each taste.

'Like Mass,' observed the Marquis. 'But then you know all about that.' He smiled, referring to my adventure in Chiapas.

The chocolate crèmes rested on a silver filigree salver, as if they were the most precious jewels upon earth.

I took the cream into my mouth and let it rest on my tongue.

Slowly, the dark chocolate seeped into my being.

I took a light bite into the crisp outer shell.

It broke gently.

I began to savour the sharp taste of the macerated fruit and the soft, velvet raspberry cream as it spread through my senses, enlivened and warmed by the surging aftertaste of the brandy. I closed my eyes and let the flavour engulf me. Taste had never lingered so long as this new richness stole into my soul.

'Excellent,' interrupted the Marquis. 'More brandy, I think.'

Mérigot stepped forward, and poured from the decanter.

'You may leave us now.'

The servant bowed and left the room.

'I have been thinking, my dear Spaniard,' the Marquis began, 'how much of our life is like unto this chocolate. We are imprisoned here, in the Bastille, as surely as this crème is secured inside this chocolate. The walls of the prison are as dark, but we are surely the crème within.'

'That is very true,' I observed, 'and the cream lies in the chocolate, as the brain lies in the body. Or perhaps,' I continued, warming to the brilliance of my theme, 'the raspberry is the brain, the cream is our soul, and the chocolate is our body.'

I was drunker than I believe I had ever been before. 'Our body . . .' I continued, 'that can snap so easily, releasing the fluids within.'

'Everything,' said the Marquis, 'all of our lives, can be explained by chocolate.'

'Chocolates are as stars in the sky laid out before us,' I observed gravely. 'Each one has its own unique identity, but all are part of the main.'

'They are both medicine and delight. We need no other food,' continued the Marquis.

We sat in contented silence.

Then the Marquis jerked forward. 'But we do need some Armagnac.'

He leaned forward greedily, but found that he could not reach far enough and slumped back into his chair. It seemed that he could hardly move.

'Mérigot!' he cried, but no answer came.

The Marquis was stuck fast to his chair.

'No matter,' he observed, although his fixed position was giving him some concern.

I remained in my seat, sparing him the humiliation of asking for my assistance. The night was still, and there was only the sound of the fire to entertain us. I yawned contentedly. Pedro stretched out by the fire and prepared to sleep.

'You are tired,' the Marquis observed, pointing at me.

'I am, but also content.'

At last, summoning one great effort, he rose from his chair. 'You can sleep on my couch if you wish. I have some work to attend to.'

'I find that I do not want to move. I could eat this meal for ever,' I replied.

'Eat. Drink. Rest. What more can we desire?' he asked, crossing the room to his desk. He then trimmed the wick of his candle, put a further chocolate in his mouth, and began to read from *L'Histoire des Filles Célèbres*.

As the fire burned brightly before me, I did not think that I had ever been so warm in all of my captivity, and I fell into a deep and contented sleep.

All the cares in the world had passed.

Peace.

Sleep.

And the memory of chocolate.

I dreamed of the dark-red blouses of the women in Chiapas, regretting that I had never made love to them. Here was my chance to capture that moment, if only within the fantasy of dream. I imagined one on either side, undressing me, and then slowly taking off their clothes. It was a hot afternoon, and they were telling me how long it had been since they had seen me, and how much they wanted to share the pleasures of their bodies. One straddled me below, while the other let her breasts fall in my face. Slowly, and with infinite tenderness and burning delight, I was about to be brought to the pinnacle of excitement, when I heard Pedro yelp sharply, as if warning me of some great impending terror. The women instantly retreated from me, seeming to vanish before my eyes, leaving me quite alone.

Furious at this interruption, and on the point of admonishing my dog, I realised that I had woken up.

Pedro's warning had been no dream.

I tried to focus on the sight before me.

Could this be true?

The Marquis was crouched naked on the ground. With the *molinillo* in his right hand, he was moving stealthily towards my dog. He established a position behind the grey-hound, and put down the *molinillo*. Then he lifted Pedro's hind legs, and began an act that I can only describe as simultaneous sexual arousal. As I finally regained consciousness I suddenly realised that the *molinillo* was about to be used for a purpose that it had never known before and that I would have to act with extreme speed if I were to prevent its insertion into Pedro's rear.

'Stop!' I cried.

'Do not interrupt,' shouted the Marquis. 'The bow is taut, the arrow is about to be fired.'

'Stop,' I cried again, but the Marquis began to rub Pedro all the more vigorously, and raised the *molinillo* in the air.

'The pistol is cocked, I await the explosion,' he exclaimed. 'Silence, you filthy Spaniard.'

I leapt across the room, kicking the vile and flatulent man to the ground. Pedro yelped in terror and the *molinillo* fell to the floor.

Black with fury, I stared down at the sprawling mass before me.

The Marquis was lying on his back, surrounded by his own blubber, all dignity lost.

But he would not be defeated.

Unable to rise from the ground, he let forth a low roar.

'How dare you!' he cried. 'You are mad. You know nothing of the ways of the world.'

'No, sir,' I shouted back, 'you have affronted all decency. You have corrupted my dog, abused my *molinillo*, and tainted the memory of the woman I love.'

'Silence is consent,' wheedled the Marquis.

'You are the vilest man I have ever known. Life is not meant to be an existence of selfish indulgence,' I cried. 'It is precious and rare and we are all responsible, one to another. We are more than mere animals. Do you not understand that?'

'Bah!' exclaimed the Marquis. 'We possess our

flesh for but a moment of infinity; we must explore all its possibilities . . .'

'No,' I cried, gathering Pedro to me. 'You cannot exploit the vulnerable. There cannot be love without responsibility.'

'Love?' shouted the Marquis. 'What do you know of love?'

'More than you will ever know,' I lied bravely, and fled from the room.

My head pounded and my throat was dry. A night of hedonistic joy had ended in vice and depravity. I felt a deep shame, and resolved that I would have to escape this desperate place as soon as possible.

For the next two weeks – or at least it seemed like two weeks though my awareness of time had now all but left me – I continued to make my linen rope ladder and avoided all contact with the Marquis. I asked permission to alter the times of Pedro's daily exercise, and was granted an additional walk each evening. This gave me time to plan my much needed escape.

It seemed that I would have to find a way of passing through three locked doors and then throw my rope out of the latrine window; after this I would have to abseil down the walls, cross the moat, and make my way east for safety. It could not be more difficult than anything I had done at sea and, with my new clothes, I was convinced that I could pass for a Frenchman.

And then, one night, as I sat on the edge of one of the small broken chairs in my cell, I heard the strangest of noises. At first I thought it must be mice or rats, and Pedro's ears cocked. But the sound seemed to be less like scuttling, and more like a low reverberation.

It was coming from my mattress.

I looked across the room. The nits, mites and moths that had been festering in my bed were now emerging from their eggs and cocoons. I was soon surrounded by cloud upon cloud of dark moths and pale-blue butterflies dancing before my eyes as they flew up towards the dim light above.

Pedro began to leap up after them, barking happily, and I only just managed to hide the ladder before I heard the door of my cell open.

It was the turnkey Lossinote, who had been surprised by the vigour of Pedro's barking.

'What has happened?' he cried.

'Look at the butterflies,' I answered with mock anger. 'How can I sleep if they fly around me so?'

Lossinote paused in amazement.

'They're beautiful.'

The room was filled with a veritable mist of quivering butterflies, the most palpable symbol of freedom, alive in my cell.

'We must catch them,' I cried. 'Do you have a net?'

'Of course not,' said my gaoler.

'Then we must use our hands, and release them through the window. I cannot sleep with so many of them around me. And, besides, what if they escape into neighbouring cells? There will be chaos. Help me and be quick about it.'

I leapt up to demonstrate how such a task might be achieved, and Lossinote began to jump forward too, clasping his hands together, amused by the new game in which he found himself employed.

He was a short, fat man, untrained in the capture of butterflies, and his face began to redden still further as time passed. It was clear that he took little exercise, and had spent much of his time in the Bastille eating the better of the food that had been destined for our tables.

After half an hour we had succeeded in catching some eight or nine butterflies, but there were still three hundred of the creatures flying about my cell.

Lossinote was panting for breath.

'We need help,' I cried.

'Nonsense,' the exhausted gaoler answered, missing yet another butterfly. 'I can do this.'

Pedro barked loudly and the gaoler stood on a chair to gain extra height. With great effort, he then summoned up all his strength, and threw himself forward into the air, making one last triumphant leap towards the butterflies passing over his head.

He missed –

and fell senseless onto the ground, his face redder than it had been in all his life.

At once Pedro bit the keys from the leather thong

at Lossinote's waist. Clasping the sheeted ladder, we quickly made our way down the stairs.

It was now or never.

I abseiled down the walls, holding Pedro tight against my side. Having been accustomed to climbing the rigging of a ship, we found the descent easy, and were soon outside the moat of that great prison. Not knowing how much time we had before the discovery of our escape, we ran from the Bastille down the Rue du Faubourg Saint-Antoine.

Our route was blocked by crowd upon crowd of people all surging towards the monastery of Saint-Lazare. They were obsessed with its destruction, and exhorted us to join them. We had no choice but to agree if we were to avoid being lynched. At the corner of the Rue de Montreuil, I was caught in a further maelstrom of citizens, some two thousand strong, all wearing red or blue cockades, carrying sticks and crying out: 'When will we have bread?'

As the crowd threatened to turn ugly, I darted down a narrow alley and banged on the first door that I could find.

'Let me in,' I cried.

'Who is it?' came a voice from within.

'In the name of all the citizens of France, I urge you to admit me. I have been a prisoner in the Bastille!'

Suddenly the door flew open.

Pedro slipped through the crack, and I was hauled inside and flung on the ground.

Six Frenchmen rose from their stools, and looked down at my broken and dishevelled body. A cacophony of accusation spat from their mouths.

'Why have you come here?'

'What do you want?'

'How dare you interrupt us.'

I looked up in helplessness.

'Please . . .' I began.

'What shall we do with him?' said another. They spoke so fast that I could hardly understand them.

Pedro began to bark but found it impossible to stop their advance.

The men then began to crowd around me. I knew I was about to suffer the greatest beating it had ever been my misfortune to endure. Looking from man to man, it appeared that there was no possibility of mercy. I had interrupted the most solemn of gatherings and must now, it seemed, be punished.

What this place was, or who these people were, I knew not. In the distance I saw a table scattered with papers. Knives, clubs, muskets, sabres and pistols surrounded me, and a woman was knitting in the corner with almost demented fury. Another was carving meat from a dried ram's head.

But then, in the corner of my eye, I noticed what appeared to be a row of china drinking vessels. They were almost identical to the *trembleuses* owned by the Marquis de Sade.

I looked at the men advancing upon me, and then back at the row of *trembleuses*.

'Wait!' I cried.

'Are you a friend or an enemy of the citizens of France?'

'A friend. Please. Let me drink some chocolate with you and I can explain everything.'

'You know about chocolate?'

'Yes. Chocolate,' I repeated boldly, without knowing what I was doing.

'What else do you know?'

'Nothing. Chocolate, chocolate, chocolate; it's the only thing I know anything about.'

'Don't believe him,' shouted the knitting woman.

'How did you know about chocolate?' asked an aggressively large man with discoloured teeth.

'It happened a long time ago . . .'

'But we only decided on the password yesterday . . .'

'What?' I cried. 'I knew nothing about a password.'

'Then why did you use it?'

'I used the word by accident. It has often helped me in my travels.'

The men looked at each other; the woman was unimpressed.

'I do not know what you wish to do. I have spent many days and nights in the Bastille, a dark and forbidding place piled with guns and weapons from which it is impossible to escape.'

'How many guns and weapons?'

'I do not know. But there are over two hundred cases of powder stored there.'

The leader stepped back.

'Powder?' He looked at his companions, and then turned to me. 'Do you think we can take it?'

'It would be hard. But I know every passage of the Bastille.'

'Monsieur,' said the man with the discoloured teeth, 'if you agree to help us then your tongue will have spared your life. To the Bastille, gentlemen. The Revolution will be ours.'

The following day I found myself swamped in the midst of a huge crowd of desperate people: carpenters, cobblers, locksmiths, tailors, cabinet-makers, wine merchants, glove-makers, hatters, defecting soldiers, gardes-françaises and gunsmiths – all the professions of Paris it seemed, and all now converging on the Bastille.

As we surged towards that dreadful institution, my heart beating hard lest I be re-arrested and re-imprisoned, the Governor sent word that he wished to negotiate with two of our number, inviting them to dine with him so that the situation might be resolved peacefully. Our spirits soared but, when the representatives failed to return after we had waited for more than two hours, we began to doubt the Governor's words, and suspected that our fellow citizens had been imprisoned.

A second set of representatives was then sent, demanding the gunpowder.

This too met with no success.

The crowd grew impatient, crying, 'Give us the Bastille!' and began to bang upon the gates. A carriage-maker climbed onto the roof of a perfume shop that abutted the prison, leaned across, and cut the chains of the drawbridge. It crashed down, killing one of our number, but the crowd surged forward. Soldiers defending the Bastille immediately opened fire, and a terrible battle ensued. Pedro was terrified. It was as if we were back, once again, at the siege of Mexico. We were surrounded by gunfire, smoke, burning carts and frightened horses. The battle seemed to last for hours, but by five o'clock the Governor displayed a white handkerchief, and the prison was taken.

The crowd stormed forward and seized all the guns and powder they could find before releasing the prisoners and shouting triumphantly of liberation. The Marquis de Sade had been moved to Charenton, and, in truth, only seven remaining prisoners emerged: old, infirm and amazed to see the light. On observing the newly vacated prison, it did strike me as strange that I had ever bothered to escape. Major Whyte tottered towards me, his waist-length beard and silver whiskers strangely illuminated by the last of the sun, and was promptly hoisted aloft and declared a hero of suffering and endurance. The crowd surged through the streets, carrying the head of the Governor on a pike, in a cacophonous tumult. The bulk of the people no longer knew who had control of the city and in the weeks that followed any attempt to clarify the situation only resulted in further chaos. Assemblies were convened, trials were established, and politicians were assassinated. Each person appeared to be testing out a new identity, erasing the past while still uncertain of his or her future character. Every day brought new possibilities and new dangers.

I had no choice but to become a citizen of France.

After burning the elegant clothes that had been ordered in the Bastille, I bought a pair of sans-culottes and changed my name to David Dieugagne. Then, having found lodgings with a small company close to the River Seine, I also secured temporary employment in the chocolate house of Messieurs Debauve and Gallais in the Rue des Saints-Pères.

Here we began to experiment with imported ingredients such as Persian salep and Japanese cachou. Convinced of the medicinal properties of chocolate, and knowing of its value in the treatment of those suffering from pulmonary diseases, weak stomachs and nervous disorders, we introduced a new range of remedies, offering a special tablet for the sick and nervously afflicted, a pastille with almond milk to soothe the stomach, and a ganache with barley sugar cream for delicate ladies. The pharmacy was filled each day with the aroma of these new creations as the scents of dark chocolate, orange flower water, ambergris and vanilla mingled with the perfume of anxious and well-dressed ladies, accompanied by small and extremely irritating Chihuahuas.

I became the friend of a baker called Simon Delmarche, who sought my aid in a plan to combine the principles of bread making with the new possibilities offered by chocolate. Anxious to make friends rather than enemies in this great city, I told him that I would be glad to help because I did indeed have certain ideas as to how this might be achieved. And so, over a period of some six months, we rose early each morning, coaxing various combinations of flour, water, almond, yeast and cacao until at last, after several disastrous failures, we succeeded in creating one of the simplest, but I must say greatest, inventions known to humankind: the *pain au chocolat*.

Back at my lodgings, I also came to befriend a small and extremely rotund Austrian gentleman, whose dream in life was to establish a series of hotels across Europe. He had arrived in Paris to purchase some of the properties that had been newly vacated by the aristocracy. Each evening we would take chocolate together before retiring for bed, and Franz would tell of the estate outside Vienna where he lived with his wife and three children. He was a kindly but other-worldly man who did not fully understand that his business interests might arouse the anger of the revolutionaries. I warned him that it was dangerous to speak loudly of his affairs lest he too be mistaken for an aristocrat, and in the weeks that followed we became increasingly concerned by the volatility of the political situation, the public distrust of foreigners, and the terrible introduction of the guillotine.

Although I was content with my work at the chocolate house, a day did not pass when I did not feel uneasy. The necessary secrecy involved in my long life had become almost intolerable. I was terrified that I would be unmasked as an impostor, that people might guess my Spanish character, and that if I ever told the truth about my condition I would be mistaken, once more, for a madman. With no means of proving our identity, and uncertain as to whether we would be believed in our allegiance to France, the time came when both Franz and I were forced to conclude that the best course of action would be to leave the city.

Sure that he could even find employment for me at one of his establishments in Vienna, my companion invited me to accompany him on his journey home. It was an offer which I could not refuse.

And so, after taking leave of the few friends that we had made in Paris, Pedro and I found ourselves travelling in the back of a comfortable carriage pulled by four chocolate-coloured Brabants some seventeen hands high. Although our future was uncertain, and Pedro persisted in licking my face and giving me anxious and soulful looks throughout the journey, I could not help but feel hopeful. Our trust in Franz would be rewarded by a safer, more fulfilling and more comfortable life. Surely our future could not be as frightening as our past?

CHAPTER 5

The estate lay close to the Vienna Woods and was well regarded both for its dairy produce and for its apricots, which were harvested each July and August. Indeed, the family was famed for the resulting cordials, brandies, compotes and preserves.

The lady of the house was a tall, dark-haired and nervous woman, as slender as her husband was portly. In fact they seemed to be the exact opposite of each other: Franz being small, blond, weighty and prone to excess perspiration, forever dabbing a handkerchief on his forehead; whereas his wife was pale, powdered and thin. Together they had produced three children: Katharina, aged ten, who performed the duties of a mother when her own was too debilitated to do so, Trude, an opinionated daughter of eight, and Edward, a troublesome and energetic son of three.

On the afternoon that I arrived in Vienna, the family was involved in the making of an apricot preserve. A wooden table had been set in the middle of the orchard and the children ran amidst the trees, selecting the fruit and placing it gently in narrow wicker trays. Pedro followed them with enthusiasm, barking happily, jumping up at them, and even, at one point, picking an apricot himself by leaping up and dislodging it with his nose as if it were a ball with which to play.

It was a beautiful summer's day, and the green of the trees stretched out before us as if an artist had laid them out on a palette: lime, verdigris, and Prussian green; emerald, pine and terre-verte.

Franz was clearly delighted to be home, and clasped his wife with unbounded affection.

'Bertha, my joy, my life, my wife.'

'You are home at last. Now I can rest,' she said. It was clear that motherhood exhausted her.

'I have returned with a charming new friend, my treasure.'

His wife broke off the embrace and turned to me.

'I am pleased to make your acquaintance,' she said guardedly, wiping her hand on her apron before holding it out for me to kiss.

She had been slicing apricots on the table, cutting them into halves, and removing the stones, before placing them into shallow white bowls. 'We are making a compote,' she announced, 'and then the children will bake a cake.'

Her husband reached down and plucked up an apricot.

'I love this fruit more than anything in the world,' he said, letting it rest in his hand, rolling it gently backwards and forwards in his palm. 'Look at its roundness and its simplicity. It is the greatest treasure we own; so short is its season, so rare its beauty.'

He held the apricot up in the sunlight.

'Have you ever seen anything with a finer glow? Look at the blush on it. Admire its colour. It is the purest of pale orange, the mirror of creation. When I see a perfect apricot I know that God is good.'

'All things mirror God's creation,' Bertha offered, and, indeed, it seemed that afternoon we were perhaps in a very Eden, surrounded by the laughter of children.

'Taste,' offered Bertha gently, turning to me. 'I will choose one for you. Hold out your hand.'

I looked into her dark eyes and she placed the apricot in the centre of my palm. The sun gave the fruit a golden halo against my flesh.

'Taste,' she said again.

I looked at her husband as if to ask permission, for to partake of such nectar might have seemed an act of infidelity, so sensual was the exchange; but he simply nodded in agreement with his wife's order and gestured that I should continue.

Biting into the soft, slightly smoky exterior, and letting the juices roll around my mouth, I was amazed by the way in which the texture of the fruit became increasingly soft, moving slowly and luxuriously from its supple skin to an intense and mellow centre.

Suddenly I could not help but think of Ignacia, the rounded plumpness of her rump, the soft liquidity of her insides, the honeyed moistness I had known.

'What are you thinking of?' Franz asked.

My mouth was full of apricot.

'Is this not the purest nectar?' he continued.

I looked at the pile of fruit before me.

'They are as pure as the buttocks of a new-born child,' I replied, hastily trying to banish Ignacia from my thoughts.

Bertha shuddered with disgust.

This observation was clearly a mistake.

Katharina smiled. 'The man says they're like your bottom, Edward.'

'No, they're not. His bum's bigger,' said Trude.

'That's enough.' Bertha shuddered once more. 'It would please me if you would refrain from such vulgar observation. We have much to do here. I have compote to produce and cakes to make.'

'I apologise without reserve,' I said. 'I meant the remark in all innocence.'

'Bum bum bum bum bum,' sang Edward.

'Quiet,' shouted his mother, but the boy laughed and sang again.

'Bum bum bum bum bum.'

'This is intolerable.'

'Bum bum bum bum bum.'

'Bertha, my darling . . .'

'Bum bum bum bum bum.'

'Why do the children always do this? No one understands how difficult I find this.'

'Bum bum bum bum.'

'No one understands anyone, my darling. We are all individuals . . . cast adrift on the waters of life.'

'Bum bum bum bum bum.'

'You are all impossible . . .' Bertha threw down her handkerchief and fled back into the house.

The children stared after her.

My friend gave chase, following his wife up the stairs, calling after her, 'Bertha, my darling, Bertha . . .'

'Bum bum bum bum bum,' sang Edward.

'In the name of God be silent!' I shouted.

'Don't speak to our brother like that,' admonished Trude.

We were in the Garden of Eden no more.

I must confess that I have never been familiar with youngsters and have not been able to understand how so much of a parent's duty lies in the presentation of a mood or emotion to the rest of the family – whether it be authority, cheerfulness or patience – which its owner does not, in fact, possess. I have noticed that this often creates both tension and distress.

And yet it appears that the production of children is the most common consolation of mortality, satisfying, at least in part, the desire to salvage a spark of ourselves to live on in future generations. I therefore decided that if I were ever to truly understand the common attempt at everlasting life I would have to befriend both these children and their parents.

The first thing to do was surely to retrieve the current situation and find some form of entertainment for the three frail specimens that now stood before me.

It was not easy.

'What shall we do now?' I asked, realising that I had made the most inauspicious of beginnings to my stay in Vienna.

'Mother will take to her bed. Father will comfort her,' Trude stated, in a surprisingly matter-of-fact manner.

'You must help us,' offered three-year-old Edward. 'Mama is sad.'

The children spoke as if a mature understanding of human frailty had been instilled in them at birth.

'What about the cake?' I asked firmly, grasping the only practical idea in my head, for I knew from the conversations with my friend that the Austrians liked nothing better than a large slice of cake.

'Do you actually know how to make one?' Katharina asked.

'Is there no cook?'

'Mother dismissed her.'

'A maid?'

'The cook and the maid were friends. They left together.'

'And so you are alone. Do you not have a governess?'

'Nobody stays here long.'

'Why not?' I said, looking at the green of the orchard before us. 'It is a beautiful place.'

Katharina looked at me as if she had never met anyone so foolish before.

'Father doesn't pay people enough, and we are too far out of the town. The girls who look after us are lonely in the countryside and do not want to marry farm workers.'

'And Mother says they are lazy,' Trude added, 'and then she cries like she did then, and we have to do everything ourselves. Why are you here?'

'I have come to Vienna in search of employment.'

'What can you do?' asked Katharina sternly.

'I write, and I speak several languages. I can also cook.'

'Are you going to be our teacher?' asked Trude.

'I think your mother would not approve.'

'Can you play with my soldiers?' asked Edward.

'Why do you have a dog?' asked Trude, accusingly.

The children seemed to want to do nothing but question me. This was a considerable source of alarm because I was well aware of the ability of children to proceed to the heart of a matter by a process of direct questioning, and was still uncertain of my abilities as a dissembler. If I was forced to tell the truth about my adventures I would not know when to stop and would be accused of corrupting them with fantasy. The only option was to change the subject and avoid further inquisition.

'Enough. We should finish making the compote and clear this away. And we must appeal to your mother's good nature through our industry,' I ordered. 'Let us surprise her with cake.'

The children were extremely hesitant, and I decided that a firm hand was needed.

'We need eggs, butter, sugar, cream and chocolate; three mixing bowls, two saucepans and a bain-marie; spoons, palette knives and whisks. We also need a well-lined cake tin. Can you find them?'

'I know where they are,' said Katharina. 'I have even made cake myself with Mother.'

'Very good; then you can help. Trude, you finish the compote, and Katharina and I will start on the cake.'

'What can I do?' asked Edward.

'You can play with Pedro in the orchard.'

'I've just done that . . .'

'Well, you can do it again,' I replied tartly. How anyone can ever live with three children defeats me.

'Separate the eggs,' Katharina ordered.

'I'll mix the butter and sugar,' said Trude.

Katharina placed a pan of water on the stove and broke chocolate into a bowl which rested just above the surface. The apricots were stewing on the side.

The production of the cake was, it must be said, a complicated process. The oven was heated, and Trude creamed the soft butter and the brown sugar. Katharina asked me to add six egg yolks, one at a time, to the melted chocolate. This she then stirred slowly, turning the mixture into a rich and dark luxuriant paste.

'Now whip the whites . . .' she ordered.

I pulled out my trusty *molinillo*, and whisked the six egg whites. The mixture stiffened and rose beneath me, frothing into frosted peaks as if they were miniature versions of the mountains I had seen in Mexico.

Trude added the butter and sugar to Katharina's chocolate and I folded in my egg whites, together with some flour.

'Now,' ordered Katharina, 'this is too heavy for me. Take it and continue stirring.'

I picked the bowl from the steam, scalding my hands, but too proud to show my pain. Katharina then held out a metal cake ring and asked me to pour the mixture gently into it. As the thick, dark confection oozed out of the bowl the pain of the burn began to surge through my hand and I was taken back to Mexico once more, to the memory of the flames as I pledged my love to Ignacia. No matter how long I lived, it would always be with me. I would take it out like a treasure, letting it roam through my head, savouring each detail: the look in her eyes, the fall of her hair, the way in which she held her head – it was a memory so powerful it could bring life to an end.

Katharina took the cake away and placed it in

the oven. The slamming door awoke me from my reverie.

'Now for the icing,' I said, almost to myself, melting chocolate once more, and suddenly sad. This was what it was like to be lost, I thought, to be detached from life, living in memory because the present could never be so alive or so vibrant again.

'Will this work?' cut in Trude.

'I am only uncertain about your oven,' I replied. 'I am not used to it.'

'How will we know when the cake is ready?' she asked.

I could not think of a response. All my confidence had disappeared.

'When the smell of baking is at its height,' Katharina replied seriously.

'And when will that be?' I asked.

'In about an hour. It is a smell which we always know. Our mother has taught us. It is then that we know that we are at home.'

At last I began to savour the aroma of the baking chocolate cake. It seeped into the air and filled the room with reassurance, as if my confidence was slowly returning. I stopped to watch the two girls pour the icing onto a marble slab, and it seemed then that perhaps the present need not be so terrible, that there could be moments in life, no matter how small, when fear and anxiety could be stilled and the pain of absence and loss could depart, if only for a while, leaving clarity and truth lying, as it did now, in something as familiar as the simplicity of children baking.

I wanted to see the cake rise, to watch the process unfold before my very eyes so that I could fix this moment in time and remember it always. I walked across the room to open the oven door in order to relish the aroma of the chocolate as deeply as I could, to watch the mixture rise up before me. All would be well.

'Don't open the door!' shouted Katharina.

It was too late.

For with these very words the mixture buckled, sagged and collapsed.

'What have you done?' said Trude, crossing the room to witness my calamity.

'I don't know.'

'It's ruined,' said Katharina, pushing me out of the way, and pulling the tin from the oven.

'You should have waited. The whole art of baking depends on temperature and patience. Do you know nothing?'

'No,' I replied.

No matter how long I lived my life, it seemed that I was destined to remain a man who misunderstood the art of timing.

'Look at it,' she cried. 'It's a disaster.'

The cake had buckled in the middle and now looked like an elephant's ear. It was even thinner than when we had first placed it in the oven.

'We'll have to start again,' she concluded.

Edward and Pedro bounded in from the orchard.

The boy looked at me sternly.

'I want cake.'

'It's only good enough for the dog,' said Katharina.

'Can it not be remedied?' I asked with an attempt at optimism. 'Perhaps we could have a flat cake.'

'No. It's useless. We will have to start again. I'll go to the hens for more eggs.'

Katharina left the room muttering a word, which I did not fully catch, but which must have been 'imbecile'.

I looked at the sad sight before me.

There is nothing more terrifying than the contempt of children.

'Try it,' said Trude.

I ripped a piece and placed it in my mouth. It was warm and leathery.

Trude now tore the cake into pieces, giving some to Edward and some to Pedro, before placing a small morsel in her mouth.

'It tastes of fish,' she pronounced.

'No, it doesn't,' I said. 'It tastes of chocolate and egg, and perhaps a little touch of leather.'

'Definitely herring,' she insisted.

'How can it taste of herring?' I asked.

But Trude would have nothing to do with me. She threw the remaining portion on the floor, and Pedro began to tear it apart.

'At least somebody likes it,' said Katharina, returning to the room with six newly laid eggs.

'Now, let's start again. Remove the compote

from the stove, and place it on the side to cool.'

I looked at the glutinous orange mixture, so dense and so rich, as if there could not be a sharper or purer concentration of apricots, and put it to one side.

Then I began to whisk the egg whites once more. As I returned to the actions of only an hour ago, and the same activity unfurled before me, it occurred to me that perhaps I would have to continue living until I learned to perform each task correctly. I would have to go on, condemned to repeat myself, again and again, until I had learned such things as never to open an oven door whilst baking. Only then might I be ready to learn about love, desire, memory, death, and all the other things that keep people awake at night.

I thought once again of my life and its past, unable to believe that this moment in which I now lived was once the unimaginable future, and that soon, all too soon, it would become long ago. And a terrible fear then struck me: the knowledge that I did not know how many lessons I would need to learn, or what tasks I must perform, before my life might right itself and I would begin to see things clearly. I had lost the nature and purpose of my quest, and was now far adrift, like a ship without steerage, rudder or anchor, with only memory to guide me.

I looked again at the quiet concentration of the children around me, at Pedro eating the chocolate cake, at life continuing in all its detail and triviality, and began to wonder how I should live my life, and what purpose would fill my days. Perhaps I would simply have to trust luck and chance, and hope that when I had learned the true nature of my fate I might be allowed to die.

These are the thoughts a man can have whilst cooking.

And so I poured the chocolate mixture into the cake tin, and again the smell of baking welled up before me. And at last, when it seemed that there was not a single space in the room, neither crevice nor corner that was not filled with the aroma of chocolate, we opened the oven door.

The cake had risen before us.

I pulled it from the heat, and placed it on the sideboard to cool next to the apricot compote.

Edward climbed onto a stool.

'Don't touch it,' cried Trude. 'Come away from there, Edward, and play with your soldiers.'

She pulled out a box of infantry and began to line the Austro-Hungarian army up against the French. Then she took a piece of thread and divided the cake into two halves.

Katharina began to prepare the icing. She placed sugar and water in a large saucepan and brought them to the boil. Then she stirred in the melted chocolate until it began to take on a threaded appearance. She strained the icing into a smaller pan, and poured the mixture onto a marble slab. As the chocolate fell, she asked me to turn and fold it with a palette knife, so that the sauce began to thicken, firm and lighten in colour.

'This is a vital moment,' said Katharina. 'Trude, bring over the torte.'

Her sister turned and let out a sudden scream. 'Edward!'

We froze in horror.

Edward had climbed back onto the stool and had covered the entire cake in apricot compote. It glistened with a new stickiness in the early evening light.

'What have you done?'

'Ape-cot cake,' he said, licking the palette knife that he had used.

'Move,' cried Trude, pulling Edward away. He began to yelp and cry, but he was at his sister's mercy as she shut him in the next-door room. 'Play in there and do not come back until we tell you.'

Edward began to wail and bang on the door, but his sisters were adamant. He was banished.

'Why didn't you stop him?' Trude screamed at me.

'I didn't see.'

'What good are you? What good do you do? Is there any point at all in your existence?' shouted Katharina.

'Are you not being harsh on your brother?' I asked quietly.

'You don't know anything about children, do you?' Katharina shrieked.

'What are we going to do?' wailed Trude.

'There's no time to make another cake. Father will be down from his rest at any minute, and Mother will be hysterical.'

'Could we not cover the apricot with chocolate?' I suggested.

'Don't be ridiculous.'

'We have no choice,' I continued, 'and if we allow the apricot to settle, then apply the chocolate . . . look . . .'

'Don't touch it . . .' Katharina shrieked again.

'No, allow me,' I insisted, placing the two halves of the cake together.

'Stop it,' said Trude, desperately.

'No,' I cried. 'I will not.'

I refused to follow the orders of children and began to smooth even more apricot compote over the surface of the cake.

'If we make this light and even . . .' I said, as calmly and as authoritatively as I could.

'Rather than sticky and messy . . .' Trude broke in.

'If we make this light and even,' I repeated, 'then we have a chance of success. Katharina, please continue stirring the chocolate until it is even thicker . . .' I ordered. 'The apricot will keep the sponge moist. It needs to be exactly the right consistency.'

Katharina looked at me sceptically.

'I hope you know what you are doing.'

'Madame,' I said, 'I may have only the fortune of the desperate to guide me, but if there is one thing in the world about which I know it is chocolate. For this dark liquid is the most perfect partner for all foods, and, employed in the correct manner, there is virtually no edible substance with which it cannot be eaten or drunk. I have only recently tested its taste with raspberries; there is no reason why it may not be equally effective with apricot. Now please let me pour the mixture onto the cake.'

The warm chocolate now met the glistening apricot, and I smoothed the thick dark coating across the surface.

'Father will never have tasted such a torte,' said Katharina, 'and it might be too much for Mother's nerves.'

Her sister looked out into the hall, as if either parent could reappear at any moment, and explained: 'You see, she is driven mad by his snoring.'

'I am sure your father will be intrigued. I am only sorry that your mother may suffer.'

'She is always anxious.'

'Has she not seen a doctor?' I asked, still smoothing the chocolate. Things seemed calmer now.

'The doctors say there is no cure for her anxiety. They give her salts and tell her to avoid excitement. Father eats for comfort, but the more he eats the less she does so.'

'And yet they love each other,' I said.

The children were silent. I was not sure that they should have been speaking so openly about their parents, but it seemed that in this house every role had been reversed.

'I am sorry for them both,' I said firmly.

At this moment Franz appeared on the stairs.

'My wife sends her apologies,' he called. 'She is unhappy with too much excitement and finds the children tiring. We will be dining in the city tonight, at one of my hotels. I hope you will join us.'

'I shall be honoured.'

Then he stopped to observe the chaos of the kitchen.

'Now, children, what have you been doing?'

'This man has made a cake,' said Katharina tartly.

'It is something by way of experiment,' I explained. 'The children have been most helpful.'

'It's very dark. And thicker than usual, it seems,' Franz observed.

He was clearly suspicious.

'Let me cut a piece for you, Father,' said Katharina.

'Very well, I will try it.'

The silver knife cut deep into the thick chocolate surface, and Katharina eased it slowly through the apricot and the sponge. After a second cut the slice was free.

Trude brought out some cream, and placed a plate in front of her father.

'What has happened to this torte?' exclaimed Herr Sacher. 'It seems so moist.'

As the cake entered his mouth a delectable melange of sensation must have spread across his palate, for a feeling of utter pleasure and surprise seemed to engulf him. It was as if he suddenly understood the meaning of the word bliss. He had never tasted such a cake before, the softness of the sponge, the viscosity of the apricot, and the crispness of the chocolate combining to create a sublime sonata of gastronomic delight.

He placed the fork down on the table, made as if to speak, but then thought better of it.

He could not do so.

To speak now would only delay further pleasure.

He scooped up another mouthful, and repeated the experience.

Only after he had taken five mouthfuls in silence could he consider the possibility of speech.

He leaned back in his chair, and brought a handkerchief to his perspiring forehead.

'This is quite magnificent,' he exclaimed at last. 'Apricot and chocolate. I never thought to combine them.'

Then he rose from the chair and beamed at his daughters.

'We must all try this torte. Katharina, cut more slices. Trude, fetch your mother. Edward! Where is Edward?'

The door was opened to reveal a red-eyed boy behind it.

'I did it, Father, and I accept my punishment.'

'Did what?'

'Put the apricot on the cake.'

'Did you, my boy?'

'I'm sorry.'

He looked small, vulnerable and defeated.

'No . . . no . . . no. It can't have been you,' his father was saying. 'It must have been Diego.'

Edward looked amazed. He could not understand how he could escape punishment.

Katharina glowered at me and said nothing, as if testing my honesty.

'It is true,' I admitted. 'Your son applied the apricot.'

Edward gaped at me in fear and hatred, as if I had betrayed him.

'What has he done now?' exclaimed his mother as she entered the room. 'What has been happening in my kitchen. Will no one leave me in peace?'

'Taste this, my darling,' her husband urged. 'The most extraordinary creation. We must take it to the hotel tonight and show it to the chef.'

Bertha took the warm and moist cake up into her pursed dry mouth. At once her expression changed, moving from suspicion to pleasure, as the rich delights of this accidental creation insinuated themselves into her very being.

'Sir,' she said, her mouth still full of cake and cream, 'this is indeed a most remarkable invention.'

'It is of your son's making.'

Mother and father looked at their small and nervous child.

His mother swooped down upon him.

'My son,' said Bertha, tearfully. 'You did this?'

'I did, Mama . . .'

Then she clasped him, I think, as tightly as a mother ever clasped a son.

'O, my darling boy, *mein Liebchen, mein Liebchen* . . .'

Edward's small head rested on her shoulder, and he looked back up at his bemused and beaming father. It was a tight, desperate and protective circle of family love, as if they were clinging to each other against the dangers of the world. This was why people have children, I realised, not to send a semblance of themselves into the future, but to put on some small armour, however frail, with which to confront the terrible insecurities of our existence.

'What shall we call it?' asked Trude.

Each member of the family tasted the cake and tried to think of a name, as if its rich moistness could provide inspiration. Edward's cake . . . chocolate surprise . . . Diego's folly . . . until at last I conjured a name from the air. 'Let it be called Sachertorte, in memory of this day and this family,' I said.

'A capital idea, my good friend,' Franz replied. 'Let us preserve the memory of our family in cake.'

His wife wiped away a tear and apologised for her former harshness.

'My nerves are so bad,' she sobbed.

'I can recommend chocolate for all nervous debilities, Madame,' I replied, 'if you would allow me to advise you?'

'Of course, of course.'

'I hope you will forgive my follies in your kitchen.'

'I will, Diego,' she said, quietly, 'with all my heart.'

And then she held out her delicate hand for me to kiss.

At last, all was well.

That night we took the remains of the cake to our dinner at the hotel, and Herr Sacher insisted that I should instruct the cook in its creation the very next morning, paying particular attention to the relationship between the moistness of the cake, the texture of the apricot, and the dark smoothness of the chocolate. We would use only the finest ingredients, and serve it with a freshly beaten, lightly sweetened cream to provide a cool finishing touch, enhancing the texture and prompting the flavours.

It was, it must be said, a triumph.

CHAPTER 6

This cake proved particularly suited to the Viennese temperament and I was soon placed in command of a small delicatessen within the hotel in order to sell Sachertorte to the general public. It was a hard winter and the people of the city appeared to wrap themselves in as many clothes as they could find, eating to excess at every opportunity, fattening themselves up against the cold. Observing them, I was able to understand for the first time the notion that we are what we eat, and realised that perhaps it should not surprise us if we feel refreshed by grapefruit, lightened by a lemon soufflé, pleasured by wine, or reassured by chocolate. In our choice of victuals we can predict our future well-being; not only in our bodies, which are comforted, filled, strained or over-burdened, but also in our minds. I began to discover that food could actually generate emotion; and that whereas certain substances might make us agitated and aggressive, others might soothe and calm. I began to study where these emotions might lie and in which part of the anatomy they were concentrated, discovering that alcohol made me depressed, eggs and cheese did not agree with my stomach (causing both fear and insecurity), whilst sausages made my face feel greasy and my body lethargic. Only chocolate offered stability and consolation.

The delicatessen became so successful that we were able to take on extra staff and I was relieved of its daily management in order to concentrate on my research. Herr Sacher was convinced that I could create further delights, and provided me with a small culinary laboratory next to the kitchens in which I could undertake a series of experiments. He asked me to pay particular attention to the creation of chocolate liqueurs which guests could savour in the smoking room after dinner, and my shelves were soon filled with strange marinades, pickling jars and fermenting fruit: raspberries nestled in crème de cassis, cherries were drenched in cognac, and prunes improved immeasurably once they had been saturated in slivovitz. I believe that I was the first to use an early form of Grand Marnier, allowing the sureness of the chocolate to mingle with the zest of the orange and the attack of the alcohol.

But, as the years passed, and my experiments grew increasingly complex, I became even fonder of alcohol than I was of chocolate. I started to drink as I worked, pouring glasses by my side as I created a Kirsch roll or filled a chocolate ball with cognac, and it eventually became clear to me that I was quite unable to cook without this necessary fortification.

After several months the addiction took hold so surely and so firmly that I was trapped before I had been able to realise what had happened.

When I walked through the streets of Vienna, in the Graben, or down the Kartnerstrasse, I blamed my longevity, my boredom and my lack of hope for this inexorable slip towards the delusive and belying attractions of the bottle. Whereas chocolate might satisfy an instant craving, I found that it made me too easily satisfied, too replete, whereas wine or brandy offered more graduated pleasures. With alcohol I no longer needed to be the prisoner of a lengthy memory and an uncertain future. I could slowly slip out of consciousness, escaping the terror of my infinite life, freeing myself into oblivion.

At first I convinced myself that this was a good thing, and sought out those who drank, recognising them in the street by the burgeoning floridity in their faces, the moments of carelessness in their grooming, and their soulful and distracted airs. After a minor setback, or a blunted ambition, these people had searched for the same desperate reassurance I sought myself. Out of fear, out of the need of courage, they had believed that drink might make them safer, happier, wittier, louder, cleverer, or simply forgetful of the pains of life.

Together with these new acquaintances, I sought out conviviality, escape from labour, licence and true freedom, little recognising that at the moment when alcohol appears to provide its greatest liberty one is most truly imprisoned by it. I noticed the sacrifices people made to purchase yet more drink, buying in small and regular quantities so that the effect might be less noticeable. In those who still retained employment I observed the over-eagerness to please mixed with the terror of discovery, whilst in those who had long lost the fight for self-preservation I could find only resignation, acceptance and the abandonment of any who sought to save them.

Perhaps my alcoholism was a slow attempt to kill myself, an endeavour to waste as much time as possible in order to end the terrible sentence of my slow life. I felt even more detached from the everyday realities of my existence, as if I was sleepwalking, haunted by memory, uncertain whether I lived or dreamed.

For although the crowds along the Kartnerstrasse seemed to understand the purpose of their lives, fulfilling their duties and their responsibilities with a grim and somewhat stoic determination, unable to live, and unwilling to die, my life was the exact opposite of theirs. I was still unwilling to live and unable to die.

The people in the streets also looked strangely familiar, even though I knew I could not possibly have met them before. It was as if they were the ghosts of people I had known in centuries past, and as they travelled through their lives, convinced of their own unique place in the universe, I could not help but think that they led an almost identical existence to those who had gone before them. Of course the world had changed, but the inherent character of its inhabitants had not.

Everything seemed both foreign and familiar. I was frequently confused, as each day now seemed to repeat itself. Sometimes I dreamed that the city was full of identical people, all moving at the same pace; at other times I dreamed that it was full of different versions of Ignacia, and that I would be haunted by each one in turn until I found my true love. In the distance ahead of me I would often see women who looked as if they must surely be her. I began to walk behind them, imagining what would happen if my instincts were correct. A woman's hair might fall in the same way, or she would have the same walk. My memory was so uncertain that I would follow these women in a trance, hardly daring to believe that I might meet Ignacia at last, excited beyond all reason at the possibility of joyous reunion and eternal salvation walking a few paces ahead of me. But each time I quickened my pace and drew alongside the woman in question, I could see that her nose was different, or that her hair fell differently, or that she wore spectacles. I was then appalled by the stupidity of my imagination. These women were but distortions of Ignacia. They were not, and never could be, her. My dreams and my despair now stretched so deeply and so monotonously across my days that I drank even more heavily.

And then, believing that life could offer no

escape from my delusions and no comfort for my despair, I decided that I would have to cease this humiliating and pointless pursuit of women in the streets of Vienna and seek a more direct course of relief from Ignacia's absence, even if I had to pay to do so.

The girl I visited was called Claudia.

I had thought of trying to find someone as dark as Ignacia, but believed that this could only make my depression far worse. It would be better to find an almost exact opposite, and Claudia was certainly that. Her most prominent characteristic was her long red hair, worn as if it had never been cut. It cascaded down her back and fell as low as her waist. She also possessed the most pallid complexion I had ever seen. It was so pale and so frail that it sometimes broke out into a rash which spread like a faded pink necklace, giving her a vulnerable yet peculiar allure; and although she was surely malnourished, poor and desperate, there was such certainty in her manner and such strength in her beliefs that I could not but submit to her strange beauty.

It was a demeaning liaison which lasted several months: she needed my money, whilst I needed her comforts, and we were trapped in an ever descending spiral of despair. I punished Claudia for her availability and for her poverty, chastised Ignacia for not being with me, and then castigated myself for my depravity. 'Is this what men do?' I asked myself. 'Is this the dark heart of us all?'

There was so little tenderness in our actions that I began to fear that I would never be able to climb out of the sordid depths in which I found myself and discover true love again, for it seemed that I had lost that most precious human quality of all – hope.

'Why do you do this?' I asked one evening after Claudia and I had again sought some form of release from our troubles.

'Why do you?' she replied.

'Out of desperation . . .'

'Then you know the answer.'

'So we are the same,' I said, realising that my time was up.

Claudia had risen from the bed and was now stooping to pick up her lingerie. She turned to look me fiercely in the eye, her nakedness brazen in front of me.

'No. We are not,' she said savagely. 'You can help yourself. You have money and privilege. I have nothing.'

She walked into a small bathing area and began to change.

'You have beauty,' I called.

'A losing beauty. The poor do not live long.'

I knew that she hated these conversations, privileged men taking a strange fascination in the poverty of prostitution.

'How long?'

'Tie up my corset please,' she asked, sitting back on the bed. 'My father died when he was forty.'

'It is strange,' I said, pulling at the laces of her bodice, 'that you should want to live and I should want to die.'

'I do not have the luxury to choose,' she replied firmly.

Feeling the lace strings between my fingers, I realised that I could either pull them as tightly as possible, or unfurl her clothes once more. I wanted to ravish her all over again and began kissing the back of her neck, pushing her down onto the bed, but Claudia forced herself away from underneath me.

'You must go. My next guest is about to arrive.'

'Let me pay him to go away.'

'No. For if I lose him, and then later lose you, I have nothing,' she said, pulling on her nightgown.

'Don't you love me?' I asked.

'How can I love you? Do you love me?'

'I like you,' I said. 'I need you.'

'But you do not love me?'

'No.'

'Then what am I supposed to do?'

'Do you hope to love?'

'I am beyond love,' said Claudia.

'You are too young to be so sad.'

'Love is rarer than you think.'

It became distressing to visit Claudia. She had closed herself off to so much of the world that after several weeks in her company I decided that

I must do something to arrest her air of sorrow and mistrust. I wanted to arouse her, to bring her back to life, to make her feel once more. Perhaps we could even redeem one another.

And so, on my birthday in early June, I gathered a basket of the first strawberries of summer and asked her to light a small fire. She told me that the room was quite warm enough and that the last of the frosts must surely have passed, but I persuaded her that the most delightful of sensory experiences awaited her.

After placing the strawberries in a crystal bowl, I began to melt a dark and bitter chocolate in an improvised bain-marie over the fire. If the Marquis de Sade had been so successful with his raspberries, I knew that I could easily match his endeavours with a fuller and more succulent fruit.

And so, as the chocolate melted, its aroma filling the room, Claudia and I slowly undressed each other, letting our clothes fall silently to the floor. We knelt down by the fire, and then began to dip the tips of the sweet wild strawberries into the warm and newly melted chocolate, feeding each other in front of the flames.

The taste was extraordinary. Our mouths were filled with the dark and bitter fullness of the chocolate and then instantly refreshed by the tender succulence of the newly ripe fruit. We kissed, rolling the taste and texture of chocolate and strawberry backwards and forwards between us, losing ourselves completely in this shared moment of hunger and satisfaction, as if we were consuming the richest, darkest and sweetest flavours that had ever been created, no longer knowing if we were taking or giving, no longer aware of where our bodies began or ended.

The room was filled with heat and flesh and chocolate. Even when we thought that we might be sated by passion, the fresh taste of the strawberries cleansed and revived us, letting us plunge once more into the dark and secret world of our desire.

I took up my pastry brush and began to paint Claudia's breasts with chocolate, covering her pale, alabaster skin with its darkness, stroking her nipples with an upward movement so that they had never been so hard or so high.

Then I began to lick the chocolate gently from her breasts. Its very thickness meant that nothing could be rushed, that this moment must seem to last for ever, as if we had been granted the secret of eternal longing. I was child and man; Claudia was both mother and lover. I could sense and even taste her milk beneath the chocolate as I sucked at her breast. We had entered a world beyond time.

At last I looked up to see Claudia's face, to find the light in her eyes, to see her happy.

She smiled fondly as she saw that both my nose and my mouth were now coated in chocolate.

Then she looked down at her breasts.

'Oh,' she said, quietly, suddenly sad, 'look.'

'You are beautiful,' I whispered, before resuming my task.

'No,' she replied, 'look where the chocolate falls, in the aureole, in the rivulets around my breasts. It shows the lines. It shows my age.'

'Let me lick you clean,' I murmured.

But Claudia took my head in her hands, and lifted me gently away.

'No. Stop now. Please. I cannot bear it. I'm sorry.'

To abandon my desire was almost impossible, yet Claudia was distracted and insistent. Once again she was struck by the strange melancholy that hovered over her, ready to possess her, offering only occasional moments of respite, so that any happiness in her life must always be fleeting.

Half-covered in chocolate, she turned her back to me and began to sleep.

'Let me rest now. Go when you are ready.'

It was over.

Even though at one point we had seemed outside time, and even though it seemed that I would live for ever, nothing of love and tenderness could last: everything must fade from me.

It was three o'clock in the morning. The fire was out and the night was cold. Rising from the bed, I cleared away the remains of the chocolate, washed the bowl, and gathered up the discarded strawberries. Normal life must resume, I thought, with all its tired familiarity.

But then, while dressing, as I turned to look at Claudia for one last time, I noticed that the chocolate over her right breast had begun to harden in the cool of the night. I stopped, watching as she slept on, unaware of my observations. The coating seemed, if such a thing were possible, to grow in perfection with each minute that passed.

It occurred to me that I might be able to make this moment last after all. I might not be the finest of sculptors who could carve Claudia's body eternally in stone, but I knew that there was a world in which even I could be an artist.

Here was my chance.

I would preserve Claudia's nipple in chocolate.

After taking a few moments to consider the exact course of my actions, and when I could bear the suspense no longer, I leaned over Claudia's sleeping body, and took the chocolate gently between my fingernails, easing it away from her breast.

I do not know if I had ever seen anything so beautiful.

Claudia turned, as if waking, and I kissed her lightly on the shoulder.

Holding the chocolate shell, which now bore the shape and beauty of Claudia's breast, I opened the door and left the room.

And, as I walked back through the streets of Vienna in the early morning light, I thought that life need not necessarily be a disaster, that small moments of beauty can be reclaimed from even the most impossible of situations, and that I might be able to create at least one thing each day, however trifling, that would make life worth living.

For it is often in the smallest of details that a life must be lived.

Unfortunately, the next time that I visited Claudia she was no happier.

'Do not wish for love from me. Do not think that chocolate escapade will make a difference to our lives.'

'I wish only that you were not so melancholy,' I replied.

'My sorrow is not your responsibility. You cannot take the cares of my life upon your shoulders.'

This much was true.

'Have you ever known love?' I asked.

'I have learned not to expect its return.'

'But why are you so bleak about the future?'

'I have seen men's minds.'

'How do you know so much of life already?' I asked as Claudia opened a bottle of brandy.

'Because I know what it is to be rejected. Because I have looked life in the face.'

'And now?' I asked.

'I try not to look at it at all. It's like staring into the sun.'

She handed me the brandy, and then began to brush her hair at the dressing table.

'Do you think that I will ever love again?' I asked.

'I do not know.' She tilted her head to one side, and I could see her face reflected in the mirror, looking back at me as I lay on the bed. 'Perhaps you will not love until you learn to think less of yourself.'

'I can hardly think less than I do already.'

'I do not mean degree. I mean quantity.'

'You mean I am selfish?'

'You told me once that you have loved and been loved in return. You are lucky to have loved at all.'

'Sometimes I can hardly remember it.'

Claudia was exasperated, and pushed her hair away from her face as an angry flush spread across her cheeks.

'You are being ridiculous. What of the love you could give in the future, have you not thought of that? Have you not thought that you might change a life?'

'No. I no longer have the confidence. I do not believe that anyone's life could be improved by mine.'

'Then why do you live?'

'I have often asked myself that question, but it seems I cannot die.'

'We all must die.'

'I once thought so; but I cannot think of it.'

'Well,' said Claudia, as she wound a black ribbon in her long red hair, 'you could always kill yourself.'

'I suppose I could,' I replied fiercely.

Claudia tied the black silk into a tight knot. She was beginning to annoy me. I did not enjoy being criticised, and she did not seem grateful for my interest. I vowed that if such conversations were to become a regular part of my visits then perhaps I should never see her again.

'Why don't you think about it then?' Claudia added. 'It would certainly put a stop to your decadent pessimism. Will I see you next week?'

She held out her hand.

'Tuesday,' I said meekly, paying her the money.

'As long as you don't throw yourself in the Danube?'

She hesitated for a moment and then kissed me softly on the lips.

'I'm sorry to tease you, my love. Try and be more cheerful next time.'

'I will be,' I replied crossly.

It was not me who needed to be happier.

Finding myself alone once more in the night-time streets of Vienna, I did not want to go home. There was so much to think about, and Claudia's words had begun to rage around my head. It seemed that we needed each other, and that, although a part of me found her irksome, I could not live without her. She had a hold on me that I did not understand.

How could I shake it off?

I stopped at a bar to warm myself and drank once more.

On the other side of the street stood a large and solidly respectable house. A Midsummer party of men and women, dressed in their finest clothes, could be seen drinking champagne and dancing together in the lighted windows of the first floor, like figures in a dream. They glided past the window, endlessly circling the room, as if they were telling the stories of their lives, waltzing towards an inevitable oblivion.

'Perhaps I could love Claudia?' I thought, attacking my third brandy of the night. If only I could learn the art of generosity and stop thinking about myself. Then I might find love again. Here it might lie, right on my doorstep.

But surely she would never love me? It would be too difficult. I would have to explain everything about my slowness, my immortality, and the promises I had made to Ignacia. I would have to tell her even more of my faults and my inadequacies, and then, even if I did manage to convince her that I was not mad, I would have to marry her, and there might perhaps be children, and it would all become horribly complicated as our lives would be lived at such different rates. I would watch them grow up and pass me. They would die, and I would outlive them all.

No, it was impossible. I could not love Claudia. It would be better to travel the world alone.

Returning to my brandy, I began to think once more about the purpose of my life.

If it was all lived in order to come to terms with death, then what was I waiting for? I had understood life's meaning, no one would miss me if I died, and I might just as well get on with it.

Claudia's words rang in my ears. '*You could always kill yourself.*'

Suicide.

That was the answer. A noble and brave end.

After all, it was good enough for Socrates.

I left the bar and walked on through the streets. A strange lightness now entered my soul. '*As long as you don't throw yourself in the Danube.*'

Suddenly my life had a purpose it had never known before. I understood that the meaning of life was but a preparation for death and that I was now heading straight into its heart.

I walked out into the Weihburggasse and listened to the bells of the Franziskankirche strike midnight – as if they were already tolling for my funeral. I then turned into the Rotenturmstrasse and made for the Marian Bridge. To die in the Danube would be a noble end. I would line my pockets with stones, and throw myself into its hostile currents.

I stopped at a small bar and drank heavily once more, persuading the barman to let me leave with an extra bottle of brandy against the cold before the dawn.

Reaching the Marian Bridge, I drained the bottle, climbed up on the low brick promontory and took a last moonlit look at the world in which I had lived for so long.

This was it.

I reached into my pocket, and found the chocolate cast of Claudia's nipple. I had no need of it now. Taking it into my mouth, I thought of

176

her for the last time. This would show her how serious I was.

I bit into the chocolate nipple, swallowed, and steadied myself on the bridge.

Come, death, embrace me.

I threw myself forward, out into the dark night air, hitting the water and spiralling down into a deep underworld, unable to see what lay below, frozen in dark waters of fear, as my body was sucked down into an everlasting abyss.

But then, as death began to close its final arms around me, I felt a strange tugging at my bow-tie, and could just discern four long legs, and the familiar cavity of a canine chest.

Pedro!

This must be a dream, a final vision of death, of life passing before my eyes?

But no! I was pulled away, up through the currents, struggling with my dog, back up through the darkness, my head finally bursting through the surface of the waters.

We swam to the bank of this great river, Pedro barking loudly, waking the neighbourhood in search of assistance. He must have travelled the night in search of me. How selfish I had been, unaware of the only living thing that shared my condition, careless of his future, abandoning him to suffer the insecurity and cruelty of inexorable fate.

Two large men now pulled me out of the water.

'What are you doing?'

'I wanted to end it all,' I cried.

'No one dies in the Danube Canal,' one of the men said dismissively.

'It is a raging torrent,' I shouted.

'No,' the other man said, 'it isn't.'

Looking back, I saw that this was, indeed, a small outpost of the Danube. In the darkness, and in my drunkenness, the realities of life had escaped me. I had not managed to jump in the right place and had then suffered the indignity of being rescued by my dog.

Into what murky shallows had my life now sunk? I could not even make a success of suicide.

The men dragged me back to Claudia's house and dumped me at the front door, just as a bearded client with a fierce look in his eye was leaving, carrying what appeared to be an artist's sketchbook.

'What have you done?' she cried. 'You are soaked through.'

The men explained what had happened.

Claudia was furious.

'You are mad to have taken me at my word. If I had known you might attempt such a thing I would never have put the idea into your head.'

'I was unhappy. I thought you wanted me to do it.'

'I was being provocative. You were so selfish and impossible.' Claudia pulled me inside and stirred up the fire. Then she began rubbing Pedro dry. 'There was no need to try and kill your dog as well. I would have looked after him.'

'He saved me,' I said.

'Well, perhaps next time you should learn your lessons of love from him rather than from me. Why did you do it?'

'I don't know.'

'You do.'

'No, I don't.'

'Well then, let me tell you. Pique. Imagined desperation. To spite me. To make me pity you. It's pathetic.'

'I wanted you to think better of me. To miss me.'

'But you wouldn't have seen my pity, you would have been dead. And now I can only believe that you are stupid.'

'Which is worse.'

'Exactly.'

'It makes me want to kill myself all over again,' I cried.

'Oh, stop that. There's no remedy in suicide.'

'But what shall I do?'

'I'll tell you what you can do,' she hissed. 'You can stop being so obsessed with your own self. You can stop talking about chocolate all the time.'

'I don't talk about chocolate all the time . . .'

'You can think of Pedro. You can think of your friends at the hotel. You can even, for once, think of me.'

'I thought you liked your life.'

'No. You like my life. I do not. That is why I am changing it.'

'How?'

'Gustav has asked me to model for him.'

'What?'

'He is going to be a great painter. He knows about love and death.'

'When did this happen?'

'We have just been discussing it. He is obsessed with my hair.'

'I'm obsessed with your hair . . .'

'He says that he is going to make me eternal. My body will live for ever through his work.'

'I do not find eternity consoling,' I advised.

'You're jealous.'

'And is he going to pay you?'

'It's a job.'

'And what will become of us?'

'We will have to be friends. You will have to talk to me.'

'No more . . . ?'

'No. No more of that. But it will be a better life. We will learn to respect each other.'

'And Gustav?'

'Will be my employer. Nothing else.'

This was a terrible shock, and my brain was so filled with the adventures of the night that I wondered, yet again, if I might be dreaming.

I tried to concentrate.

Claudia had been given the opportunity to escape her plight and was determined that nothing must ruin her. If I wanted to find pleasure in the delights of the body I would have to let her go and seek such comforts elsewhere.

It had been an eventful night.

CHAPTER 7

One dark November morning – I forget the year, but it was on one of those early winter days when the sun never seems to rise before it sets once more – a kindly Englishman with sad eyes and mutton-chop whiskers arrived in our hotel. He carried a large package and, after he had taken his morning coffee, and approved most heartily of my Sachertorte, we fell into the most interesting of conversations. For it so happened that his parcel contained a new kind of press which, he informed me, would revolutionise the making of chocolate. It could extract up to two thirds of the fat from a cacao bean, producing a dark, rich and pure chocolate powder which he called cocoa. This was then pulverised, mixed with alkaline salts in order to improve its miscibility, and beaten into a concentrated paste. The result was a soft but sweet form of solid chocolate.

I could hardly contain my excitement at this discovery. Now, for the first time, it might be possible to create an actual bar of chocolate.

In the next few weeks Mr Fry and I were inseparable, experimenting with the many ways in which this pulverised cocoa could be combined with butter, sugar and water to create these solid strips or bars. We spent hour upon hour in my laboratory, staying up so late at night that I almost forgot to drink. We were engaged on a proper enterprise at last, a project which could define the purpose of our lives.

I do not think that I had ever been so excited about the prospect of work. Each morning I rose with renewed determination, desperate to solve all the problems that lay ahead of us, resolved to create a form of chocolate that the earth had never witnessed before.

In this task I was also much supported by Claudia's enthusiasm. She seemed, at last, to be happy.

'This is the future,' she said firmly, 'chocolate for all; not just the privileged and the rich.'

'It will be completely different, I agree,' argued Mr Fry. 'We will make a taste that was once the province of the elite a common pleasure. I only worry that the gratification may be too instantaneous.'

'Like sex without love?' asked Claudia.

'Indeed,' Mr Fry responded a trifle uneasily. 'For the principal advantage of chocolate is that it cannot be taken at speed. It asks you to take time, to consider, to pause.'

'I agree,' I replied. 'It is best enjoyed in silence by people who love each other.'

'Of course, not everyone can do that,' answered Claudia.

'That is true. And yet I do not know a rich man who is happy,' Mr Fry observed. 'Even the most contented is too afraid for the loss of his wealth.'

'And do you know how to be happy?' I asked.

'I certainly know that there is no happiness in desire.'

'No,' said Claudia, giving me a strange look.

'Then where is happiness?' I asked.

'I do not know,' Mr Fry said kindly. 'I am neither a priest nor a philosopher. I am simply a businessman who makes chocolate. All I do know is received from study, prayer and observation. There are few rules in life, even when you have lived as long as I' – and here I resisted the temptation to interrupt him – 'but I believe that the greatest unhappiness often results from those times in which we think solely of ourselves.'

Mr Fry was a Quaker. He was a kindly man with bushy eyebrows, sallow skin and gentle blue eyes. He had spent his whole life living and working with chocolate, being the third generation of his family to work in the field. I realised that if the earlier part of my life had been different I could have known his grandfather when he was a boy.

As we worked together, Mr Fry confided in me that he had begun to import and manufacture chocolate as an alternative to alcohol, which he considered to be one of the greatest of evils on earth.

'Such suffering,' he observed, 'such pain, such delusion. We are here on earth for so short a time. Why do so many people spend so much time trying to forget that we are here?'

'Loneliness,' I answered, 'fear of failure. Desperation.'

I thought of Claudia, and of how much she had taught me.

'You can always redeem yourself,' Mr Fry offered. 'It is never too late.'

'To stop drinking?' I asked.

'Or to listen to the promises of Christ.'

I remembered why we had first travelled to Mexico, and could not help but think of the hypocrisy of our conquest.

'It is hard for me to have the faith of which you speak,' I answered.

'And why is that?'

I could not answer such a question. I had seen such violence and so many of the cruel accidents of fate. I had witnessed the powerlessness of humanity. I had seen how fragile and how temporary mortality must necessarily be and I had experienced the random nature of sudden death. And, having lived so long, I did not find the idea of everlasting life a comfort. I had glimpsed its reality, and the assurance of an extended life beyond our own seemed not so much a paradise as a purgatory in which we were condemned endlessly to repeat our lives without the necessary knowledge to change our mistakes or advance our understanding.

'You do not believe in God?' asked Mr Fry.

I hesitated.

What did I think now of religion, of the Catholic faith into which I had been raised?

'I feel that faith has left me; religion has abandoned me.'

'You do not fear damnation?'

'No. That is the one thing in which I definitely do not believe,' I answered sadly. 'There is punishment enough upon earth.'

'It is hard that we should suffer so,' Mr Fry agreed quietly. 'But what is life without faith; what hope is there then?'

'I do not know,' I answered. 'I lead a bereft life, as if perhaps I had already died and failed to notice.'

'I think we know when we die,' said Mr Fry simply, grinding away at his cacao beans.

He was lost in his work, filled perhaps with abstract thoughts of life, death, philosophy and good works. For he was a noble man, proof perhaps that there could be strength in gentility.

And even though he was most definitely a businessman, wealth was not his primary concern. Indeed he sometimes avoided the most profitable of possibilities, commenting specifically on the exploitation of many plantation workers who picked cacao. He refused to endorse slavery, and did not buy from the plantations of Portuguese West Africa. The good must make a stand, he

186

argued; the virtuous man must do nothing that might weaken his integrity.

He also insisted that I abandon the making of liqueur chocolates, and that my only salvation lay in total abstinence from alcohol.

'You cannot continue in this manner,' he told me. 'Something has to change.'

He repeated the idea that chocolate taken on its own could be used medicinally. It should be the drink of choice for those with decayed health, weak lungs and scorbutic tendencies.

'Chocolate,' he argued, 'is the true drink of consolation.'

I resolved to follow his example and join the temperance movement.

It was not an easy thing to do. The abandonment of alcohol made my life even more interminable as time stretched slowly before me. I was now so awake, adding some two or three hours to my consciousness each day, that I found the prolongation of my waking hours a terrible torment. I wanted less time in the day rather than more.

After four weeks of constant observation, and assured that I was making progress, Mr Fry announced that he must return to the family firm in Bristol, England, in time for Christmas. He told me, in the strongest of terms, that he did not like to leave me alone with the temptations of the bottle. Chocolate was surely the cure for my addiction and he would be happy both to provide employment for me in his factory and keep a fatherly eye upon me if only I would accompany him.

He looked so kindly upon me that I felt that I would have to agree. But fear filled my being.

What if I let Mr Fry down? If I fell into debauchery once more? He would be so disappointed.

My life now seemed to be one of dread, in which the future offered only fear. I had lost so much of my confidence. My fate seemed like a wave, far off in the distance, and I did not know how large it was or the speed at which it was coming to meet me, but I knew that it was there, that it would break all over me, and that there was nothing I could do to escape it.

It was the first time in my life that I had turned down the prospect of adventure.

Mr Fry was extremely disappointed, but told me that he felt in his bones that he was sure to see me again, and insisted that there would always be a welcome for me in Bristol if I should ever change my mind.

He left the hotel with his chocolate and his press, shaking me by the hand and kissing Claudia upon the cheeks, telling her that she was one of the most admirable women he had met in his life.

We waved him away energetically, and my heart was filled with sadness. Turning back into the hotel after his carriage had receded into the distance, I looked at Claudia.

'I think he has taken a shine to you.'

'Are you jealous?'

'Of course not,' I lied.

'You should be,' she said boldly, and then added quietly, 'Perhaps we should have gone.'

'We?' I asked.

There were times when I just could not understand her.

CHAPTER 8

B ecause Claudia spent so much time in the company of artists ('Secessionists', I think she called them), I had need of new friends, and now spent much of my time in the kitchens of the hotel with Antonio, the chef. He was something of a philosopher, a well-read and handsome Italian who was keen to draw comparisons between the art of cooking and the meaning of life.

Antonio's principal belief was that we should not expect too much from our existence but simply seek out that which is good and pure and true, taking our pleasure from the natural combination of the finest ingredients available to us. Such a philosophy was universal, and could be applied equally to food, to friends and to work. He believed that only those who know how to savour each ingredient, recognising its meaning and its purpose, could ever understand the true benefits of life. We must appreciate order and pattern in cooking, learning the sequence in which each constituent part is added, acknowledging, and then knowing in the very fibre of our being, the way in which each flavour mingles with that which surrounds it. If we can but understand how such sapidities relate to each other, and appreciate the time they need to blend in order to create a richer and deeper taste, we can perhaps begin to understand not only the nature of cooking but also the art of living, and even, he believed, the harmony of the spheres.

One day, Antonio required my advice on the creation of a suitable ragout for a wild hare that had been caught in the Vienna Woods. He was convinced that the addition of chocolate to the sauce might produce an extraordinary combination of flavours. Being an expert in the creation of the none too dissimilar *mole poblano* myself, I could not see how he could fail.

Happy to watch and advise, I did, however, feel somewhat strange when observing his cooking in detail. For Antonio possessed an enthusiasm and an energy that I had long since lost, and as I studied his preparations I could not help but notice that he was so much faster than me in everything he did. Perhaps age was creeping up upon me at last?

'Everything can be explained by the culinary life,' Antonio observed as he sliced onions, diced carrots, halved chillies, and crushed juniper berries at speed. 'We must live our lives as if we are following the rhythm of the ragout.'

The onions were cooked first, on a low heat until they softened and became a pale gold. Then he stirred in the carrots for two to three minutes, before adding, in turn, six tablespoons of celeriac, ten peppercorns, three cloves, two bay leaves, five crushed juniper berries, two garlic cloves, a quarter of a cinnamon stick, and sprigs of rosemary, bay and thyme.

'Listen,' he said, and we stood in silence in the kitchen. 'The tremor of ragout on a low heat should be like the sound of distant rain.'

And, indeed, we stood as if we were sheltering from a storm, so warm had the kitchen become as Antonio added burgundy, stock, and, at last, some grated chocolate to his culinary delight.

'This will be our finest creation. Wild hare in a chocolate sauce with chestnuts. I will serve it with dumplings. Look how the flavour rises up before us,' Antonio said, coaxing the ragout, persuading each ingredient to reach its full potential. 'Delight in each scent. Let these sweet flavours reach out to embrace you.'

I leaned over the pan.

'You must distinguish every subtlety,' he continued, stirring the mixture and adding tomatoes, 'for if you cannot, you can be neither chef nor connoisseur. Furthermore, you will never understand food, people or even life itself. For this ragout is the truest and the richest symbol of the complexities of our existence.'

I looked at him in terror.

'I cannot smell anything,' I said.

'What?'

'I must have a cold. I have lost my sense of smell.'

'How can this be?'

Antonio fetched the most pungent items he could find: ginger, garlic, basil, and chocolate. He placed them under my nose in turn and asked me to inhale deeply.

It was to no avail.

Disaster had struck.

I was unable to shake off this condition for the next four days, and became terrified that I might be damaged permanently. I considered the olfactory nerve to be the primary nerve in the body and shuddered to think what might happen if my sense of smell should disappear; perhaps my sense of taste would also be lost to me for ever? Never again would I be able to savour the aroma of newly cut grass or the first woodsmoke of autumn. The scent of rosemary, bergamot, lavender or frangipani would be unknown to me. Apples stored in a loft would become a distant memory. I would even, and here I shuddered, forget the scent of chocolate, and with it, perhaps, the memory of Ignacia.

What could I do?

After two weeks in which nothing had improved and despair filled my soul, I made my way to Vienna General Hospital. Here I was shown into the rooms of a well-dressed and serious doctor. He seemed surprisingly young, perhaps some twenty-eight years old, and was of solid build, possessing a dark beard and a waxed Kaiser moustache. He shook my hand firmly, inquired what was the matter, and began to examine my nose with brisk efficiency.

He then asked me to distinguish between certain aromas, submitting each nostril in turn to oil of cloves, peppermint, and a tincture of asafoetida from which I was expected to detect the aroma of garlic.

I could still smell nothing.

'Is this common?' I asked.

'You have anosmia,' he answered, shining a narrow beam of light into my nose. 'It is not uncommon.'

'There are other cases?'

The Doctor examined my second nostril.

'I can think of a patient who would be interested in your condition,' he continued in an animated fashion, 'a poet who wore no cologne *so that he could smell women better*. He then lost all sense of aroma himself, so guilty did he become with his olfactory infidelity to his wife. Simply by smelling other women, he was, he thought, unfaithful.'

'Extraordinary.'

The Doctor laid aside his torch and looked me in the eye.

'I have been thinking that it is sometimes the mind that triggers illness. Have you been unhappy?'

'I have not been happy for a long time.'

'And you have concerns, anxieties, bad dreams?'

'I do.'

'Sometimes the balance of nature is upset,' he said. 'Let me feel your pulse.'

I gave him my right arm and his attentiveness changed from routine familiarity to utter concentration.

'I have never felt such a pulse,' he said. 'It is about one tenth of the normal rate.'

'It has been so for a long time.'

'How long?'

I could not tell him. It was too complicated. I wanted him to concentrate on my nose and nothing else.

'As long as I can remember. But it's the fact that I cannot smell anything at all that is giving me the greatest concern.'

'Very well.' The Doctor then opened a silver canister and picked out a white powder between his fingers which he placed on the back of his hand like snuff.

'What is this?' I asked.

Without answering, the Doctor leaned over the back of his hand and snorted the white powder into his right nostril. He repeated the action with his left nostril, and then tilted his head back, sniffing profusely, as if he was trying to force the powder deep up into his nose.

'Please do the same,' he said. 'You will find it remarkably pleasant.'

I placed the powder on the back of my hand and began to snort, rocking the back of my hand to allow each nostril to benefit from its power. I felt my senses numb, as if I could no longer feel my face, and a strange lightheadedness spread through me, as if I was separated from the world.

'You can lie down,' suggested the Doctor. 'I will observe you from my chair.'

I lay down on the couch and stared at the stucco patterns on the ceiling.

Nothing seemed to be happening.

But then, after perhaps some ten minutes, I felt a slow welling sensation in my head. It seemed to build and build, until I found myself sneezing as violently as I had ever sneezed in my life.

Taking out my handkerchief to blow my nose, I was now aware of the vaguest sensations: linen, air from the window, perhaps even the leather from the Doctor's chair.

'Is it working?' he asked.

'I think that it is. Can I have some more?'

'I will prescribe some for you.'

Everything around me now began to smell of soft furnishings.

'Better?' the Doctor asked.

'I cannot thank you enough,' I replied. 'Everything seems so much sharper, so much clearer.'

'Happy?'

'Yes, I am . . .'

I hesitated. There was something about the way he looked at me. It was as if he didn't quite believe me, as if he knew that there was something more.

'This is not all, is it? Tell me . . .'

I will never quite know why I broke down at this

moment. Perhaps it was because I felt so peaceful on the couch. Or perhaps it was because I sensed this man would understand why I felt so lonely, so depressed, and so unable to find any comfort for my misery.

'Oh, Doctor . . .'

I could hardly speak.

'Often the presentation of a small complaint is but the precursor to the discussion of a deeper malady,' he told me kindly. And, indeed, it was true. For the restoration of my sense of smell had only exaggerated the subterranean malaise of my unhappiness.

'I have recently travelled to Paris and Berlin,' the Doctor continued, 'and there have been some most interesting advances in the field of cerebral anatomy in these cities. If you would like to talk further about this I would be happy to see you in my rooms at the Sühnhaus, on Maria-Theresienstrasse.'

There was something about this man's sincerity and intelligence I felt that I could trust. Here at last was a person who might listen to me, believe me, and even cure me of the strange detachment I felt in life.

And so I found myself walking into a series of rooms in one of the most beautiful houses in Vienna. The Doctor had recently married, and his wife showed me into a small study in which they hoped to establish a private practice.

'Before we begin, and before I can say anything

or analyse your condition, I must know a great deal about you,' the Doctor said firmly. 'I must ask you to lie on the couch. I will sit behind your head, and out of your vision, on that chair. Then, when you are ready, we can commence. Please tell me what you know about yourself.'

'I don't know what to say or where to begin.'

'Do not worry about the beginning. Imagine perhaps that you are in a railway carriage, and you see moments of your life flashing past. Tell me what you see.'

'I do not know. It all comes at a rush. If I am on this train of which you speak, I do not know where it is going or if I will ever be able to alight . . .'

'Lie down,' urged the Doctor.

I moved over to a low couch covered with an Iranian rug. It was even more comfortable than the one in the hospital.

'How is your nose?' asked the Doctor kindly.

'Much better,' I replied. 'I was so afraid. How can it have happened?'

'An infection probably . . .'

'But for so long?'

'I read a paper recently,' mused the Doctor at last, 'in which it was suggested that nasal illness is frequently prompted by masturbatory activity.'

What was he talking about?

'Close your eyes,' he continued.

I could not think of anything to say, and a long pause then ensued. The couch was extremely comfortable and I wondered if I might fall asleep.

Only the possibility of one of my terrible dreams kept me awake, for to be observed dreaming was something that I could not countenance.

'I do not know what to say,' I protested. 'I have never done this before.'

'Then let us start with a few facts. What is your profession?'

'I am Diego de Godoy, notary to the Emperor Charles V, and now the licensed creator of the famous Sachertorte in the hotel of my benefactors, Franz and Edward Sacher,' I replied.

'And when and where were you born?'

'That is a difficult question to answer.'

'Why?'

'Because I fear that you will not believe me.'

'Anything that is said here is between ourselves. You need not fear me, and I can assure you that you will not surprise me.'

'I do not want to tell you.'

'Very well. Would you like to tell me how old you are?'

'I cannot.'

'Do you have parents still living?'

'No.'

'How do you remember them?'

'My mother died when I was a child. My father when I was twenty.'

'And so you are alone?'

'I think so.'

'And you are Spanish?'

'I am.'

'And you have travelled much?'

'I have. I began this life as a conquistador.'

'You discovered gold?'

'And chocolate,' I added, somewhat distractedly.

'I see. Caca rather than coca.'

'What?'

'I'm sorry. A little joke.'

Was the man mad? I could not understand how the Doctor could cure me in this way, nor did I really know the disease from which I suffered. What could it be? Thinking hard I realised that it must surely be a combination of melancholy, bad dreams, and eternity. But would this man ever believe me?

'What are you thinking now?' he asked. 'I would like you to say whatever comes into your head, without fear of offence or censorship.'

'I do not masturbate,' I said firmly. There was at least one thing that I needed to make clear.

'Everybody masturbates,' the Doctor countered.

'I can assure you that I do no such thing.'

'Then how do you find relief?'

'I think of other things.'

'You can achieve satisfaction by will-power alone?' he asked.

'I can . . .' I said firmly.

'You are not married?'

'No.'

'Have you known love?'

'Long ago.'

'How long ago?'

'I do not know.'

'How old are you?' the Doctor asked.

This was becoming ridiculous. I had to help him. Even if he did not believe me, perhaps at least he might find me entertaining.

'I think perhaps I must be three hundred and eighty-seven years of age.'

'And do you know anyone else to have achieved such an age?'

'Only my greyhound Pedro.'

'Your dog?'

'Indeed.'

The Doctor seemed remarkably unsurprised by my assertions, and I was impressed by his calmness.

'And can you think why this should be?' he asked kindly.

'I do not know. All I know is that we seem to be travelling the world in search of love and chocolate, and that we might never grow old and never find rest.'

'Your pulse is certainly slow . . .'

'Like my life. I cannot live as others.'

'You think that you are doomed to live eternally?'

'I think that this may be so.'

The Doctor paused for a moment, staring into space. I turned to see if he was still listening, and finally met his eye. His concentration and intensity seemed ferocious.

'One can only prepare for life by preparing for death. If the threat of death is removed, then life ceases to have meaning.'

'That may be so for you, but it is painful to me. I no longer know the purpose of my quest.'

'You feel that you are on a quest?'

'This is how my adventure began.'

'Tell me your story. The quest is important.'

'It may take days, weeks, or even years.'

'Please,' said the Doctor, 'I think that I may be able to help you . . .'

'In what way?'

'I too am something of a conquistador,' he continued solemnly, 'but my travels are perhaps far further . . .'

'Where have you been?'

'Everywhere and nowhere. My adventure is in search of the treasures of the mind.'

'I no longer recommend adventure,' I replied, thinking of all the trouble it had caused me.

'On the contrary. I think that we must confront our fears. There is no stranger land than the human mind.'

'And no land more terrifying.'

'Then,' concluded the Doctor, 'let us explore this strange territory together.'

And so, from that moment on, I proceeded once a week to the Doctor's rooms in order to tell him the story of my life. Although we formed an uneasy alliance I soon began to depend upon my visits, storing up the right things to say, planning each encounter as my life unfolded before him.

I tried to keep my account as factually accurate as possible, but the Doctor soon began to interrupt me, asking specific questions about what he called my interior existence, the subconscious life of the mind.

'Tell me,' he asked one day, 'of what do you dream?'

'Sometimes I do not know whether I am dreaming or living my life,' I answered. 'I feel as if I am like the man who dreamed a dream in which he dreamed that he was dreaming.'

'Continue . . .'

'I cannot trust that anything is true. At times I feel that I have been in places before but do not know how or when or why. I feel that I have already lived this part of my life but can do nothing to stop it happening again.'

'We are often condemned to repeat . . .'

'What can I do? Do you believe me?'

'I believe, that whether your life is a fantasy or whether it is real, it makes no difference. It is real to you.'

'Will I be cured?'

'I hope so. For it seems you have neither the will to live nor the means to die.'

He paused to let the import of his words take effect and I noticed that he had arranged a collection of ancient burial figures on the mantelpiece: Greek vases, Abyssinian heads, Chinese horses, the Egyptian god Ptah, a Roman Venus; there was even, I was sure, an Aztec idol.

'Where did you find those?' I asked.

'I have started to collect them,' the Doctor replied modestly. 'Perhaps you recognise them?'

'I do,' I replied. 'I was there. In Mexico. I know I was.'

The Doctor picked up a small terracotta head. 'I am interested in the idea that they have only been preserved because they have been buried for so long.'

'Like emotions.' I smiled.

'Or memory, which is often past desire. Perhaps you could tell me how far back in time you can remember? Is there perhaps a recollection of when you were happiest as a child?'

'You know that I do not know if this is a real memory,' I replied. 'It is like an echo heard from far away. Memory is uncertain to me and I do not trust it. It is never stable. I think that I change a memory each time I recall it, so that although it seems fixed, it is altered, or even combined with other memories in the process of its recall. Nothing is permanent.'

'Please continue.'

'In this dream, or memory, I am a small boy, sitting in an orange grove. I have just climbed a tree, and I am resting. I am not sure if I will ever be able to get back down, but I am trying not to think about that. I am looking down over the city of Seville below me and in the distance.'

'And you remember this?'

'I do, and I feel it to be absolutely true, but it cannot be so, for the tree would never have been high enough from which to see the city.'

'Perhaps you have combined a view of the city from the hillside, with the act of climbing the tree. Two distinct memories have become one.'

'That is perhaps the case.'

'And you have made yourself seem higher than the rest, set apart in your dream.'

'I have. It seems that life exists differently for me than for other people. And it is true that I have been set apart.'

'Do you ever feel that you have divine tendencies? That you might be a type of super-man or Christ-like figure?'

'No, no,' I replied. 'That is quite wrong. It is not like that at all. And, besides, I have come to the belief now that there is no God. How can there be when there is such random suffering?'

'I agree,' the Doctor exclaimed eagerly, and our conversation now moved at an increasingly brisk pace. 'God has been invented by civilisation as a consoling response to the crushingly superior force of nature.'

'We cannot bear the thought of our extinction,' I said quickly, warming to my theme, 'and so we create another world, another stage on our journey. We see the universe not as it is, but as we wish it to be.'

'It is our escape from the chaos of history.'

'We hope for a better life beyond our own,' I said.

'Which does not exist,' said the Doctor firmly.

'I cannot believe that it does, or that there is a benevolent creator active in the universe, no,' I agreed.

Here at last was a man who understood me, and our conversation continued at a breakneck pace, as if, here, we were allowed to express what could not be spoken lest it shock the polite society of Vienna.

'God has been invented to take away the pain of death. But if you then take away God . . .'

'You must take back death,' I said.

'Exactly,' answered the Doctor. 'Now we are getting somewhere. For this is what you cannot do. This is your problem and your neurosis. You refuse to mourn.'

'But I truly believe that I cannot die, and that I must endure a living death, condemned, like the Wandering Jew, to roam the world for ever.'

'You are a remarkable man,' the Doctor replied.

'No,' I said firmly, 'I am not. I feel that I am a relentlessly ordinary person who happens to have one special attribute. I do not feel superior to other people, but detached from them.'

'Because you cannot die?'

'Exactly. I might as well live selfishly, entirely for my own enjoyment.'

'And what stops you from doing this?'

'I think that one cannot live an exclusively

hedonistic existence. Even if I live on, the pleasure must pass. It will die, even if I do not,' I argued.

'But with other human beings, pleasure seems to be a headlong rush towards death.'

'Yes,' I replied, 'it is almost as if there are people who have a death instinct. For without the will to die, there can be no will to live.'

'And without death there would be no philosophy.'

'But what then is happiness?' I asked plainly.

'I do not know,' said the Doctor, the pace of our conversation slowing at last. 'I thought that you, having lived so long, could tell me?'

'Perhaps it is truly the art of living with the knowledge that we must one day die.'

The Doctor nodded sagely.

'And this is part of our happiness?' he asked.

'It must be so,' I replied. 'We cannot be happy without a knowledge or anticipation of death.'

'I too have been thinking of these things,' the Doctor replied. 'Our only contentment in this life is but transient pleasure. We seem to love the things that vanish away. Death is the only permanence.'

He rose from his chair and walked towards the window.

'And since we have no hope of any lasting success,' he concluded, 'we must learn to live with despair. But tell me, how do you find comfort?'

'I travel. I perfect the art of making chocolate. I take comfort where I can.'

'There is nothing wrong with chocolate. It gives great pleasure.'

'It reminds me of the love I have lost and cannot seem to find again.'

'You wish for your love through chocolate. It is understandable. It is how you remember Ignacia. There is nothing wrong in this.'

'I cannot do anything else.'

'It is a sign that you love her. Chocolate is often found in dreams. My daughter dreamed of it last year. Her mother came into the room, throwing a handful of big bars of chocolate, wrapped in blue and green paper, under her bed.'

'Why?'

'Because she had been denied them earlier in the day, and so sought the fulfilment of her wishes in her dream.'

'Are all dreams so clear to you?' I asked.

'No, not all. And in your case they are often confused because of the length of your life and the complexities of your memory. But tell me,' he inquired, 'you must also be wearied by the everyday business of living if your life is lived so slowly?'

'I am ineffably bored by it, I must confess. It is hard to feel alive when life has no urgency.'

'Then you must work. Perhaps write of your experiences so that you might preserve your memories and find meaning in them. For our task is surely to understand something of the riddles of the world and try to contribute to their solution.'

He rang the bell to send for my coat, for it

208

seemed that the logic of our argument could proceed no further.

'Although I do pity you,' the Doctor consoled me, 'I can only suggest that you continue to search for meaning.'

'It seems pointless.'

'You cannot lead a retrograde life. You must push forwards, taking your place in the development of our species, and then, perhaps, death will come. You must live all you can. Live and eat and love and suffer and hope to die.'

'But I cannot seem to do these things as other men do,' I said, putting on my coat.

'You can.'

'No, I cannot. For it seems that I cannot love and I cannot die,' I almost wailed.

The Doctor put a comforting arm around my shoulder.

'Are you certain of that? Do you not feel older than you were?'

'It's so hard to know the truth of what I feel.'

Tears filled my eyes.

'Perhaps you are simply destined to live your life at a different pace. You suffer, not so much from eternity, as from slowness. You live under a greater shadow than others do, but the end will surely come. It must.'

'But what shall I do until then?'

'You must work and you must love. Work and Love. They are the only guides we have, and without them the human mind falls sick.'

CHAPTER 9

I wanted to talk to Claudia about these conversations but was convinced that she would cut my musings short with her customary impatience. She was easily irritated by what she referred to as my dream-like distractions, and could not understand what it was like to live life as I did. Yet despite our differences she was still my one true friend; and it was my fondness for her that caused my life to change, and eventually move forward onto a new and better path in the most extraordinary manner – so much so that I can say now, looking back on that time, that if there has been one person in my life who has been selfless in her care for me it is Claudia.

One cold, wet, and dark night, just before Easter, she insisted that we attend a concert in which a friend of hers was singing a Lacrimosa. I was extremely unwilling to accompany her, particularly when she informed me that the piece of music was part of a Requiem. I did not want to think any more about death, or be upset by my confused thoughts on the nature of eternity, but Claudia was insistent. I only agreed on the understanding that afterwards there might, at last, be an opportunity to talk seriously with her about these things.

And so we found ourselves in the midst of the Stephandom waiting for orchestra and choir to fill its cavernous interior. People huddled in their chairs, wrapped against the cold, and candles spluttered under the marble statues.

At last the music began. It filled the air with grandeur and assurance, proceeding with a grave and natural inevitability, as if there had been no beginning and could be no end, each phrase beginning before its predecessor had finished, building its harmonies with a daringly slow serenity. It seemed as if there could be no other music than this, as if it had been written by a man who could do anything. Each time I thought the fullness and the richness of the harmony could not possibly be more poignant or more beautiful, the music flowed on, naturally and effortlessly, into a dimension of which I could not even have dreamed. The basses sang out as if they never needed to take breath, the high sopranos as if they were dancing with their voices, echoing the frailty of humanity against the deep bass of the world, crying, 'I am here. I am part of this. I am involved in it all.' I had never heard joy and pain so combined, as if everything it meant to be human was contained within it. It was complete. Nothing could be added or taken away.

And, as I looked at Claudia, her eyes gleaming in the candlelight, I was overcome by an almost inexpressible sadness. I could not accept that this music must end; that all things must perish from under the sun.

I knew that Claudia would have to grow old, and the thought suddenly terrified me. She was living her life at such a different pace to my own, and would be here on this earth for so short a time. I tried to imagine what she would be like, and her skin seemed to shrink in the dim light before my eyes. Her face aged, and for an instant she seemed seventy years old. I was filled with horror at the speed of my imagination, as if reality was falling away from me once more and I was about to plummet, yet again, into a terrifying dream.

'What are you thinking?' Claudia whispered.

'It doesn't matter.'

'You look strange.'

'I was afraid.'

I could not help but stare at her.

'Of what?'

'Of the moment not lasting.'

'It never does,' she whispered as the music continued. 'That's the point. It is only beautiful because it is rare.'

And I thought that even though Claudia might live a long life, and have children, and eventually die so that others might come in her place, there would never be anyone like her again, that this moment could never be repeated or reclaimed. Everything created could only be lost. Despite life's beauty, whatever its securities and strengths, its transience infected the lives of all whom I loved.

To see Claudia grow old and suffer and die was something I could not bear. I would be bereft, and could not, did not, want to imagine such a thing.

The *Dies Irae* began. I had never heard anything so fierce or so destructive. Such anger and vengeance, thundering through the cathedral, filling it with terror.

I could not bear it.

I had to leave the city.

And so, terrified by my own feelings, longing for my own death and yet appalled by the very idea of the demise of my friends, I hastened to the Berggasse and explained my fears to the Doctor.

It seemed that there was no alternative but to begin the new life in England that Mr Fry had offered a few years before. It was the only course of action that would enable me to retain my sanity.

The Doctor smiled at me, as if he had always suspected such news.

'Still you refuse to mourn.'

'I cannot bear to. I know that I am fleeing my responsibilities, but I am filled with the need to escape the fears of life and the terrors of death.'

'But if you live in dread, then you must die every day. Will you work?'

'So hard as to forget myself.'

'I only warn you that your fears must and will return.'

'I know. But I shall work hard to protect myself from them. It is all I can do.'

'I think there is still much to be done before you

find peace.' The Doctor shook my hand warmly.

'Remember: we must all realise our place in the world.'

He assured me that I could always return to see him in Vienna, and that although he was sad to lose me as a patient, he recognised (adding this with a twinkle in his eye) that I would outlast a good few doctors before my time came. He also informed me that, despite his natural fear of trains, he would be glad to wave me a fond farewell at the railway station, for he would be most interested to observe a man of my slowness embracing the speed of the iron horse.

All that remained was to explain my decision to Claudia.

I drank a large cognac to steady my nerves and rang the bell of her apartment.

'Who is it?' she called from inside.

'It is I.'

She opened the door, pulling her nightgown around her.

'Have you been drinking?'

'No,' I lied. 'There's something I want to tell you.'

'You can come in for five minutes.' She held open the door and allowed me to pass. 'Sit on the chair.'

She looked so beautifully pale, untouched by time.

'There's no need to stare. What do you want?'

'Could I have a drink?'

'No, of course not. You can have some water if you are thirsty.'

'Please.'

I believed that the best thing would be simply to splutter out my news and then leave the room as quickly as possible.

It was not going to be easy.

Claudia poured water into a glass by the bed and looked at me suspiciously.

'I hope you haven't done something stupid,' she threatened. 'You look ashamed.'

She handed me the glass, bending towards me so that for a moment I glimpsed her breasts close to my face.

I closed my eyes.

I do not think that I had ever felt so uncomfortable.

'Well?' Claudia asked.

'I am going to England,' I said, quietly, my voice caught in my throat.

'Oh . . .'

There was no going back.

I had spoken.

The new-born truth filled the awkward silence between us.

'For how long?'

'I do not know.'

Claudia seemed shocked.

'Why do you want to leave? Are you tired of your life in this place?'

'No, it's not that exactly . . .'

'You're tired of me?'

'No, no, definitely not . . .'

'Our life?'

'No. It's not that . . .'

'Then why go?'

How could I explain myself?

'I feel that I do not know enough of the world. I have so much to learn. I believe that Mr Fry might guide me, and help me free my life from fear.'

'What are you afraid of?'

'Apart from you?'

'Don't be silly.'

'You know the things of which I am afraid.'

'I do.'

So many silences, as if we could not say more without hurting each other.

I looked down and noticed Claudia's bare feet.

Their soles were wrinkled, like patterns in the sand left by the outgoing tide.

Age.

'You are quite certain you must do this?' she said at last.

'I am.'

'And when do you leave?'

'Next week.'

'Well then, if your mind is made up . . .'

'It is. I'm sorry.'

'It's of no concern of mine. It's your life,' she added abruptly.

I could not understand her. Suddenly she did not seem to care at all.

'I had better go.'

'Yes.'

'Good night,' I said, but Claudia was looking out of the window now, across the roof of the opera house and out, far away, into the night sky.

My departure fell on Palm Sunday, and the city was covered in snow. The railway station was crowded with people, the tracks were cleared, and there was nothing to stop Pedro and me travelling through a wintry and frozen Europe to seek a new life in England.

The Doctor busied himself finding porters for our luggage, securing a crate for Pedro in which he was obliged to journey. In a particularly kindly gesture, he had brought us both a travel rug as a leaving present.

Claudia was dressed in her fur hat and coat, and stood uneasily on the platform, stamping her feet against the cold. I can still see the wisps of breath emerging from her mouth as she spoke, the fierceness in her green eyes, the crisp red lines of her lips.

'Well then,' she said at last, 'this is goodbye.'

She held out her hand for me to take.

It was such a cold gesture after all that we had shared together.

'I will miss you,' I said, kissing her gloved hand. 'I cannot thank you enough for all that you have done for me.'

'And I must thank you. Will you ever return?'

'I do not like going back,' I said, thinking of Mexico. 'It is never the same.'

'Then shall we never see each other again?'

'Come and see me in England,' I said, as brightly as I could.

'Perhaps.' She sounded unconvinced, and dropped her hand.

We looked at each other in silence. We had shared such companionship that it was impossible to believe that it might be ending.

'I am sorry to see you leave. You set me right.'

'You have been a true friend,' I replied, clasping her warmly. 'You have been as a sister to me.'

She swallowed.

'Yes,' she said, 'I suppose you did think that.'

I could hardly hear her words, and our bodies seemed awkward together. Something was wrong. Claudia would not look me in the eye.

'What do you mean?' I asked.

'Nothing, nothing. Our love would never have survived in any case . . .' she said quickly, as if wishing as soon as she had spoken that she had not said such a thing.

'Our love?' I questioned, letting my hands drop. 'What do you mean "our love"?'

'You did not see?'

'What should I have seen?'

'That in the end I loved you.'

'My God,' I cried, 'but you let me talk and talk and talk . . .'

'It was part of loving you.'

'You kept silent for five years?'

'Yes.'

'And what about Gustav?'

'He is my employer. I do not love him.'

'And now it's too late? For us?'

'That is why I am telling you now.'

'Why didn't you say so before?'

'Did I have to spell it out?'

'Yes, of course,' I said. 'You know how slow I am.'

How had I failed to see what was happening to us?

'Come,' said the Doctor, walking towards us from the baggage car. 'You must board the train.'

Claudia knelt down and held Pedro's head.

'Look after him,' she said to this beloved greyhound. 'Your master cannot survive on his own.'

'I will always remember you,' I said.

'And I you,' she replied, standing up once more. 'At least I learned to love again.'

The Doctor led Pedro away and placed him in a small crate ready for the train.

'Was that really love?' I asked.

'I think it might have been. We knew each other. We felt safe with each other. We were protected. It was better than desire.'

I reached out and held Claudia to me, but her body felt stiff, as if she did not want to touch me. I could not believe that I had failed to see what stood before me. Was I destined to spend my life in ignorance of the truths that surrounded me?

'You think I do not know what love is?' I asked.

'I cannot know what you think. I only know that it seemed right to me.' Again she could not look me in the eye. 'I felt safe, for the first time in my life.'

'Then should I stay?'

'No. It's too late.'

'I could change my mind.'

'No,' she said sadly. 'I do not think that it would be right. I am loved less than I love.'

And then she stopped, as if she could not contain herself any longer.

'You didn't even think to ask me . . .' she said quickly, her voice breaking, 'to come with you . . .'

The guard blew on his whistle. The carriage doors began to slam shut. How many passengers on this very train, I wondered, were frightened of the journey ahead, reluctant to leave their past and their securities?

Steam poured around us. The wind swept Claudia's hair across her face. She clasped her handkerchief tightly, as if she was angry with herself and with the wind.

'You must leave.'

She was crying now.

'Try to find happiness,' I said, holding her shoulders again.

'If only it were so easy.'

'It may be easier than you believe.'

'No, I don't think so. I don't think that it is.'

'I'll never forget you,' I said.

'And I'll always love you,' said Claudia sadly, 'even if you are the most selfish person I have ever met.'

'Come,' called the Doctor once more.

CHAPTER 10

I spent ten years in England. Although Mr Fry had become an old man, his company now stretched across the streets of Bristol. Every year extra buildings were converted from slum tenements in order to house the storing, roasting, winnowing, crushing and squeezing of cacao beans in order to make his famous concoction. Together we improved the process of manufacture still further by mixing and rolling the chocolate in a conching machine, reducing the size of the particles in order to create a new smoothness, rocking the mixture backwards and forwards for up to seventy-two hours at a time.

It was a complicated and painstaking process. In order to ensure uniformity of both colour and texture, Mr Fry and his sons had discovered that we needed to temper the chocolate. This was done by raising the heat of the cocoa mass to some one hundred and fifteen degrees, and then slowly lowering it over a large bowl of ice so that the crystal nature of the fat could be destroyed. We then re-heated the mixture for just under a minute, until the temperature reached eighty-nine degrees, and at last produced a hard and wonderfully glossy chocolate.

'Temperature is everything,' the elderly Mr Fry observed, looking at me seriously. 'And do you know why?'

'I do not.'

'Because the melting point of chocolate is only slightly below the temperature of the human body. That is why it melts in the mouth as soon as it is placed there. Never forget temperature, Diego,' he continued as if a professorship in chocolate had just been invented and he was its first incumbent. 'Taste, Temperature and Texture should be your watchwords in its creation.'

And so each day, after the morning service in the factory, Mr Fry and I would taste chocolate together, as if it were a replacement for the Christian communion that I had ceased to attend. After a few months, we could almost judge a chocolate by touch alone, but we proceeded with the strictest of tests, wearing white gloves, and keeping a glass of ice-cold water by our side to preserve the acuity of our palates.

Thus we evolved the best method for evaluating our creation.

First we would examine the chocolate by eye, checking the evenness of its colour. There had to be total consistency and no bloom. Then we would test the 'snap'. For chocolate should break cleanly, like a small section from the bark of a tree;

and finally we would place each specimen in our mouths, and time the melting.

Our evaluation was a slow, savouring process, in which we explored the 'mouthfeel', measuring on our pocket-watches how long the flavour remained. The finer the chocolate, the longer the finish.

I learned so much from Mr Fry that I had almost become an Englishman, knowing when, and how often, to keep silent, restraining my emotions, keeping my own counsel, and even wearing uncomfortable and impractical tweed clothing. He was truly my patron and taught me the abiding laws of friendship; and that this life which seems so long is, in fact, lived in an instant, and that we must one day be judged not so much by a divine figure as by the far more frightening prospect of our own, elderly selves.

'Friendship,' Mr Fry declared, 'and respect. Follow these ideals and you will die a happy man.'

Then he stopped as if struck by a sudden random thought.

'For we should die as we have lived. Think of a blue vase filled with anemones. Watch it change over so short a time. See how the flowers open, bloom and decay.'

It was as if he was about to cry.

'They die so beautifully. That is how we must leave the world when our time comes, as naturally and as gracefully as possible.'

Some people carry an aura, as if they are rarely troubled by the trivialities of everyday existence. I hesitate to use the word 'holy' but I do believe that Mr Fry was such a man.

And yet . . .

After I had spent some ten years in his employ, Mr Fry became blind and his health began to fail. Unable to work further on his utopian dream of restoring the centre of the city, he became increasingly frail. I knew that he must die, but could not accept this inevitability, and was overwhelmed, yet again, with the fears that had struck me in the cathedral with Claudia. I simply could not bear the prospect of his impending death.

I would be alone once again.

The thought filled me with dread.

I had to escape these feelings.

And so I come to another point in my life for which I can only feel embarrassment and shame.

The more I thought about my past, the more dreadfully it seemed I had behaved. I could not face the truths of life. I could not stare it in the face as Claudia had done. Inconstant, selfish, wilful, and frequently drunken, I could not find any justification for the length of my existence.

Falling into yet another of my black despairs, I could only seek further escape from the realities of life. Removed from the immediate sphere of Mr Fry's fatherly influence, my imagination, my dreams and, it must be confessed, my self-obsession now took control of the very fibre of my being.

I began to gamble.

Each night I crept away from the factory and joined a group of card players in a Bristol coffee-house down by the docks, involving myself in cribbage, poker, whist, bridge, and gin rummy. I drank ruby port and consorted with all manner of unruly characters as we hazarded our fortunes upon the tables.

I knew that this was wrong, and that the Quaker doctrine specifically forbade such activity, believing it unprincipled to gain by other people's losses, but I was desperate to escape both the mortality of my friends and the length of my eternity. Recklessness became my creed. Money was of no concern, and I lived each day as if it were my last.

After considerable initial success I began to bet on anything: how long it would take a woman to cross a road, the chances of rain in the next three days, or the likelihood of Queen Victoria lasting another year. It was the only excitement in my life, and I viewed every event in terms of risk, living in a perpetual world of 'What next?'

Even though I sustained heavy losses at the table, I was convinced that I could always win more money back. I was, in a way, invincible, for I would eventually outlive any who played against me. This longevity gave me a confidence and a daring which amazed all who saw me.

But as my debts increased I was forced to borrow money from a fellow gambler, Mr Sid 'The Nose' Green, a stocky Londoner who seemed happy to accommodate my needs. He was a practical man with gaudy tastes, being particularly partial to yellow waistcoats, possessing not a morsel of self-doubt in his body, and owning one of the loudest voices I think that I have ever heard. He offered me all the lines of credit that I might need.

'The Nose' seemed initially unconcerned at the large sums he was lending me (at an interest rate of some twenty-five per cent per annum) and only became keen to reclaim his money when he required a large sum to invest in a new business activity. And so, one dark night, at the end of a particularly difficult game of poker in which I had failed to anticipate the royal flush of an opponent, my creditor leaned over, and whispered in my ear: 'I require the return of four hundred pounds by Monday.'

'What?' I cried out loud, and then checked myself in a whisper. 'You know I cannot honour such a loan.'

'There can be no delay.'

'But I have not the money to repay you,' I hissed.

'Then it will be the debtors' prison at best or vengeance at worst.'

'But you are my friend.'

'A businessman has no friends.'

'Mr Fry is my friend,' I argued.

'That dying philanthropist? Don't make me laugh.'

'I cannot pay you what I owe.'

'Then you must do the only thing that you can do to save yourself from a life of poverty and desperation.'

'And what is that?'

'You must stand me your greyhound.'

'What?'

'He has a long stride, and should be good on the bunny after three hundred yards. He could be the dark horse I need.'

'What are you talking about?'

'Racing, my Spanish friend. Greyhound racing. Your dog could be hot if he pings the lids.'

I was amazed by his belief in Pedro's prospects, and could not accept that any good might ensue from his involvement in such a race. But I also could not avoid the sad fact of my indebtedness.

I would have to agree to the demands of The Nose.

And so, reluctantly, but in a mood of some desperation, I took Pedro on a series of long runs on the downs around Bristol. I thought of all the times that we had shared together, of how long we had lived, and what a friend he had been. I was asking him, once more, to save my life.

It was strange to see the manner in which he was regarded. I had bought him a special coat, and passers-by admired his sleekness, even commenting that he looked a 'sleek-headed little racer', and 'a decent stayer'.

I was so proud. I had taken him on as a puppy, and now here he was, elegant, graceful and, it seemed, eternal, ageing at an even slower rate than I was myself, perhaps a tenth as fast, for whereas people took me to be a man between forty and fifty, they assumed Pedro to be some eight or nine years old.

And then the great day arrived.

'We'll have to change his name, of course,' said Mr Green when we arrived at the racetrack. 'He can't just be called Pedro. The name's too short.'

'What name had you in mind?'

'Spanish Lady.'

'He isn't a lady.'

This gave him pause.

'What?'

'Didn't you notice?'

'No, of course not. I've only seen him running in the distance, shooting after rabbits in the woods.'

'What about Spanish Gold?' I suggested.

'Very good,' he replied, 'you're beginning to get the hang of this. Ten pounds on him and your advance is paid if he wins. I'll even lend you the money,' he added in a conspiratorial whisper.

'I will take no more money from you,' I said sternly.

I was determined that from this moment on, no matter how long my life, I would neither drink, gamble, nor live on credit: for in these three things lies the greatest cause of our unhappiness upon this earth.

And yet how often had I vowed this, only to break my promises?

As the excitement mounted, Pedro was given a green and red racing jacket and examined by a veterinary surgeon who placed a muzzle over his mouth. This was not a popular move with Pedro, but I was assured that this was to prevent snapping and biting during the race (a form of sportsmanship from which I was sure that Pedro was immune).

All the dogs paraded before the public, and were then led from the paddock area down to the start.

Pedro eyed me with extreme suspicion as I placed him in the trap. Perhaps it reminded him of being crated on the long train journey from Vienna. He was resentful of being enclosed, especially since he had led a life so devoid of canine company and was now being denied the opportunity to frolic with the five other greyhounds with whom he was to compete: Fleet of Foot, Gothic Knight, Mercury Breeze, Sweet-Toothed Parisian, and Jackpot Glory.

The race was about to begin, and the January air was full of frost, tension, and the sharpening comfort of hip-flask whisky. I stood beside a large American in a full-dress business suit smoking a Corona-Corona cigar.

'Have you got a dog?' he asked.

'I have.'

'My money's on Sweet-Toothed Parisian. She's been knocking on the door for a while and is hot to crack at this grade.'

'I think Spanish Gold might win,' I said tentatively, but before the American could reply, a gun was fired, the traps were freed, and the dogs were chasing after an artificial hare, mounted on a roller skate, and pulled by a windlass.

The dogs approached the first bend in a frenzy, front down, backs up, and with their tails wagging furiously. I could see Pedro straining every muscle as the patently false hare raced ahead.

'Go, Pedro, go!' I cried. 'Come on, Spanish Gold!'

'Get on the bunny!' shouted Mr Green.

After three bends the dogs were closely bunched but Pedro broke free of the pack with a sudden surge of speed, and raced with the most majestic stride ever a dog strode, flying towards the finishing line with a grace of movement that amazed all who saw him. There was no question that he was the finest dog in the race, and indeed, he went on running, chasing the hare as it reached the end of its pulley, intent on its destruction.

'What a dog!' cried Mr Green, as he slapped me on the back. 'I've made a fortune. You should have listened to me.'

'I hope I can claim him now.'

'Certainly not. There's plenty left in his locker. I've entered him for another race in half an hour. Get him ready.'

'That's a fine dog of yours,' said the cigar-smoking American. 'I think I'll put some money on him in the next race.'

'Please don't,' I said. 'I would not like you to lose it.'

I was fearful for Pedro, and did not like to see how profusely he had begun to sweat.

After drying him off with a towel, I rubbed a little mink oil into his coat, and gave him a small amount of fresh water.

He was panting heavily and his eyes had lost their lustre. How could he possibly race again? He needed rest and looked to me for aid.

But Mr Green was insistent.

'I've put five pounds on him,' he said. 'You could move into credit if he wins again.'

'I do not think he has the stamina,' I replied.

'Nonsense,' said Mr Green.

'Look. He's so weary.'

'How old is your dog?' asked the American.

'I do not know,' I replied, truthfully.

'We must have him in the race,' said Mr Green. 'He has top billing, and the money's pouring in.'

'Do I have to?' I asked.

'Yes, if you want to avoid the debtors' prison.'

My head was filled with confusion but it seemed that the only chance of redemption lay in placing Pedro in the traps once more.

His life too was doomed to repeat itself. The traps were lifted, the crowd roared, and the dogs raced away.

Pedro was hemmed in at the first bend. By the second they had bunched so tightly that it was hard to tell which greyhound was which and Pedro was straining every sinew, head to head with Sammy's Day. Neck and neck, stride for stride, breath for breath, the pair raced towards the finishing line; it was impossible to tell which dog might win, so desperate were they both to gain the prize. At times Sammy's Day edged ahead, his head low, mean, and determined, but as they neared the final bend, Pedro leaned to his left, taking the inside as sharply as he could, breathing hard and accelerating away. And, as they approached the finishing line, Pedro, with one last supercanine effort, seemed to take off and leave this earth. His whole body stretched and lurched, as if it had never been so long, leaping over the line as if his body might never land, on towards the disappearing hare.

The crowd were wild with excitement, cheering Pedro's achievements, and he stretched his legs as if he could run for ever. I truly believe that no one had ever seen a dog run so fast or stride so bravely, but, as Pedro rounded the track once more, bemused by the disappearance of the false rabbit, and as if engaged in a strange lap of honour, a sharp pain took hold of his being.

Desperate to continue, but unable to do so, he bravely ran for fifteen or sixteen more strides until finally, as if there were no more breath in his lungs, he lay down on his side, gasping, not only for air, but for life itself.

I was filled with terror.

Pushing my way through the heaving crowd, I raced across the track and threw myself against his frail body.

'Pedro,' I cried.

The crowd jostled around me.

'Let me alone,' I cried, looking down at the panting form beneath me. 'Leave me alone with my dog.'

The American offered Pedro some chocolate, as if it were some kind of divine restorative.

Pedro licked it uncertainly, looking up at me for guidance, unsure that he could trust an act of such generosity. He seemed like a seven-year-old child in all his love and faith in me.

'I'm very sorry,' the American was saying. 'He gave you his all.'

I spoke as if in a dream.

'He was my only friend. He was all I had in the world.'

'I know.'

I cradled Pedro in my lap. The American stroked his head.

'It seems that I have known him all my life . . .'

'I know . . . I know . . .' The man leaned forward and kissed Pedro on the head. 'But it's time to let him go.'

There was nothing I could do but wait for Pedro's breathing to cease. He looked up at me as if offering an infinite sense of forgiveness. Exhausted by life, perhaps now, at last, he had found comfort in death, and was ready to take his leave.

This was surely the beginning of the end for us both.

And then.

At last.

It was over.

I stood up, cradling Pedro in my arms, never having known such emptiness. Looking up at the dusky sky I wanted to howl with grief. I no longer knew where I was or what I was doing, and was possessed with blankness, as if I had lived a thousand years in which not a day had counted or made a difference. A wall of isolation wrapped itself around me. The crowd seemed to part, and I left the stadium, alone, with the only friend who had stayed with me across the centuries, as if he were the child I had never had.

I walked onto the Bristol downs and dug Pedro's grave, making it as deep and as wide and as soft as I could. It was so hard to lift him and to hold him; he had never liked being carried, and now that I had his lifeless body in my arms, I could understand why he had resisted such dependency for so long.

Climbing down into the grave, I could not bear to place him in it, cover him with earth and leave him there. He felt so cold against my hands.

I recalled all the times we had shared. I remembered how we had lain side by side at Ignacia's grave, unable to move. It seemed so distant a memory now; so much had crowded in upon our lives since that terrible discovery. Yet these two deaths now united to form one distinct feeling of loss, an intolerable absence of love.

I stood over Pedro's grave and began to weep.

My life was bereft.

This, then, was mourning.

It was unbearable.

I decided that I could no longer stay in the city, for everywhere reminded me of the former happy times I had shared with Pedro.

Taking my leave of Mr Fry, and having been relieved of my debts to Mr Green, I boarded a railway train for London. There I thought that I might forsake all adventure and try my hand at the serious and sober profession of banking.

It was the seventh of May nineteen hundred and six.

Imagine my amazement, therefore, when I found myself seated on the train opposite the American who had shared my misery on the racetrack.

'Sir,' I said, 'I am delighted to see you again.'

'The pleasure is mine; although I am sorry to see that the marks of sorrow still lie heavily upon you.'

'They do, but the sight of you enables me to ease my pain, though I doubt it will ever disappear. What brings you to this train?'

'I have business to attend to in London before my return to the United States.'

I knew that it was considered impolite to ask a man about his business and could think of nothing more to say. We sat in silence as the green of the English countryside passed before our eyes.

'You know,' the man said, 'I owe you a great debt.'

'I have no creditors,' I said.

'I mean, a debt of ideas . . .'

'I think you must be mistaken.'

'Indeed, sir, I am not.'

Although the man had a cheerful face he seemed reluctant, almost nervous, to continue our conversation.

'I see you do not wish me to speak,' he said. 'I must leave you to your grief.'

'No,' I said quickly, 'pray stay. I want for company and have always been afraid to be alone.'

'We are all alone,' he said sombrely. 'We must have fortitude.'

I thought of asking him if he was a Quaker, but stopped myself, weary now of moral debate.

'There is something that I must tell you,' the American continued.

My attention lurched back into the present.

'Something for which I must seek your permission,' he was saying.

'And what is it? Ask any favour, and if it lies within my power I will gladly give it, for I will always remember your act of kindness to my dog.'

'It is your dog about which I need to speak with you.'

He reached into his pocket and placed a small lump of chocolate on the table.

'This is chocolate from the bar I gave to your dog when he was dying. Look at it,' he continued.

I was suddenly reminded of the mould of chocolate I had taken from Claudia's nipple.

'It has a strange shape,' I said tactfully.

'It marks the last lick of your dog.'

'So it does.'

'I think it should be preserved,' he said.

'How?'

'I will make chocolate in that shape.'

'You make chocolates?'

'Indeed I do, sir, and I know you to be an employee of Mr Fry and a connoisseur of such matters. I confess that I have followed you for the past few days, learned of your plans, and wish to offer you employment in my company.'

'This comes at a rush, sir,' I replied. 'Are you serious in your proposition?'

'Never more so. Sooner or later there is likely to be a war in Europe and it is important that you, as a foreigner, leave England. Come and join me in my factory.'

'And you will make chocolates in this shape?' I asked.

'The memory of Pedro will be preserved for ever. I will make the finest chocolate drops that have ever been made, solid at the base and rising to the narrowest of peaks.'

'Then, sir, I will always be grateful to you. Please, make this chocolate. Your tender-heartedness to my dog will rest long in my memory. The stroke of your hand, that final kiss.'

'A kiss,' the American said quietly.

And then, as the train headed towards London, we gradually told each other the story of our lives.

My new companion lived in a large Pennsylvania town dedicated to chocolate. He possessed twelve hundred acres of dairy farm, and I was to be housed and fed according to my status. He then gave me a letter to provide to the immigration authorities and informed me that if I should take the *Mauretania* the following month he would be pleased to organise my future employment. I would work in his factory and be happy at last, for it was in labour, he believed, that the true definition of a man's purpose and identity lay.

Although I was delighted to secure employment, it seemed too good to be true. I had learned to distrust such hopes, for it still seemed that whatever promises, allurements, and kindness might fall my way in this uncertain and lengthy life, traps, delusions, and false enticements still lay forever in my path.

Having passed through London I walked along the coast at Tilbury, where I thought once more upon my future. Heavy clouds formed around the weak glow of the setting sun, and a thick mist began to roll in from the sea as it met the River Thames.

I picked up a few shells, and reflected again on the length of my life, its slowness paced against the accelerating mortality of my friends.

If my life was a river, I thought, then my past must lie all upstream, rolling out to be lost in the sea. But the tide was on the turn. The Thames was full of whirlpools, eddies and strange currents, as though the future of the sea was meeting the river of the past. Caught in that exact point of the turning tide, it then seemed that everything was held together in one conflicting moment, and that nothing in my life was simply past, present, or future. It was all one continual watershed.

A comet blazed in the distance.

Would I still be alive when it visited the earth again?

CHAPTER 11

After paying six pounds to travel in the steerage section of the *Mauretania*, I found myself sharing a cabin at the front of the ship with five boisterous men who smoked and spat profusely. This was far from ideal, and over the next few days I tried to avoid them wherever possible, making a lonely and secret trespass onto the higher decks.

The boat was a floating city, weighing some thirty-three thousand tons, and had become home to over two thousand passengers and eight hundred crew. There was a ballroom, a swimming pool, restaurants, promenades, and an Italian smoking room, all spread out over five decks, linked by a grand staircase.

It could not help but remind me of when I had first crossed the Atlantic, missing Isabella, sailing for over a month, fearful of my future and infatuated by my desire. How small such concerns seemed now, how distant those dreams. Did that past really belong to me? Did such memories have any meaning? I had spent so much time in a distracted state that I wondered again if I had perhaps been absent from my own life.

The journey lasted seven days. I managed to avoid the temptation to gamble on the lower decks, and ventured frequently on the promenade, where I heard myself described as 'the man who walks alone'.

There were so many people: gentlemen playing quoits; children swimming in the pool; yet more ladies with small dogs.

One morning I stood for hours watching a boy flying a kite over the sea.

It seemed so simple and so timeless.

I thought of the sounds of the words *kite* in English, and *Ewigkeit* in German: eternity.

On the very last evening, as I watched the richer diners proceed towards the grandest of the restaurants, anticipating their Chantilly soup, braised oxtail, or galantine of capon, I chanced upon two women who had observed my evening *paseo*. They were clearly intrigued by my demeanour.

'Are you lost?' the taller of the two inquired.

'In life, or on this ship?' I asked abstractedly.

'Either,' answered the taller.

'Or both,' said the smaller. 'You look so alone.'

'I was seeking a place of quiet and solitude . . .'

'Well then, we must not disturb you . . .'

'No, no, I would be glad of your company,' I replied hastily.

The women had a comforting aura of kindness about them.

'Then please join us for dinner. You have a detached but inviting air,' insisted the taller woman.

'I am not sure if I am permitted to join you.'

'Nonsense,' the smaller woman insisted. 'We shall dine with whom we please. And it pleases us' – she fixed me sternly with her gaze – 'to dine with you.'

'Very well,' I replied. 'I would be delighted.'

The ladies could not have been more different. The tall, willowy woman wore an exotic oriental dress and a cloche hat pulled low over her forehead. The smaller had her hair cut short and wore a long kimono with a heavy Chinese chain of lapis lazuli.

'We are Miss Toklas, and Miss Stein,' said the shorter woman. 'Or Pussy and Lovey as we call each other.'

'Although you may not do so,' said the thin woman, whom I took to be Miss Toklas.

'I am delighted to make your acquaintance,' I replied as the waiter pushed in my chair.

We ordered the food and the women took great delight in the array of miniature mushroom tartlets, herrings in oatmeal, and caviar blinis on offer.

'Very munctious,' said Miss Stein.

'This will be quite delicious,' observed Miss Toklas.

'Pussy collects menus. She is the most wonderful cook, aren't you, my cherub? Lovely hard-boiled eggs with whipped cream, truffles, and Madeira wine. Chicken liver omelettes with six eggs and cognac. It's all extremely goody.'

'Don't go on, fattuski,' Miss Toklas replied.

'I am also Mount Fattie,' said Miss Stein. 'That is what she calls me. And Alice is my lobster wifie.'

'I will tell no one,' I said, and smiled.

'You do not seem happy,' Miss Stein observed, laying out her napkin as if her remark was the most natural thing in the world.

'I live a restless life,' I replied.

'Have you ever felt love?'

'You ask very personal questions, Madame.'

'They are the only ones that are interesting.'

'Then I will try to answer them.'

'Pray tell.'

'It was a long time ago.'

'And you were happy?'

'I think that I can truly say that I was.'

'Then you must go back. Go back to when you were last happy and start again.'

'I am not sure if I can.'

'Time moves on and people say that we should live in the moment, but I believe we can only define ourselves through love.'

I groaned. Yet another person was telling me to find happiness in love and work. If only it were that simple.

'Mortality is nothing if it cannot stand the wear and tear of real desire,' Miss Stein pronounced.

'It is terrible to think of it,' I shuddered.

'Have you ever stopped thinking long enough to feel?' asked Miss Toklas.

'Someone to love is something to live for,' said Miss Stein.

It was clear that these women were determined to proceed to the heart of things and that I could not escape their beady questions with mere politeness.

The main course was served.

I had chosen wood pigeon with chestnuts and cabbage; Miss Toklas ate a rabbit pie, while Miss Stein began her lobster with beurre blanc.

And gradually, as the meal progressed, I felt an extraordinary calm fall upon me. It was similar to the slow enjoyment of chocolate, so smoothly and unexpectedly did this peace descend. I suddenly realised that I could trust these women with my life; they had such a likeness for loving. And so when they asked to hear my story for the second time, I felt that I could not refuse them.

It took an hour to tell. Others might have thought that the longer I spoke the more certifiable I must be, but these women listened attentively and with compassion throughout.

'A sad tale's best for winter,' said Miss Stein when I had finished my story.

'And yet I feel my life will never end,' I said, quietly.

'I am sorry to say this, but the solution is simple,' argued Miss Toklas. 'You must either kill yourself or return to where you will find love.'

'I have tried both,' I said sadly.

'It seems that you live in a continuous present, and that your life is a hymn of repetition, endlessly encircling itself,' observed Miss Stein. 'Repetition. Repetition.' Her thoughts seemed to drift. 'We are condemned to repeat our lives and our mistakes until we improve ourselves.'

'All that I have improved is chocolate.'

'Yet that is no small thing.'

Miss Toklas looked at me sternly.

'And how have you improved it? By loving it. By caring for it. You must do the same with life.'

'Even when it wearies me?'

'It is then that you must care for it most,' concluded Miss Toklas.

'Remember the volcano that you climbed in Mexico,' said Miss Stein. 'It seemed dead. Hollow. Exhausted. You mounted its sides. You saw the great city before you. It may have been destroyed but now it stands there again. The volcano can erupt at any moment; it can burst into life. Rekindle the flames. Erupt again. You have been dormant too long.'

She clasped my hand tightly, with a desperate urgency.

'I see its dark gold. Feel the heat. Be the volcano. Explode into being.'

The waiter was watching us.

'Would you like dessert?' he asked. 'We have an excellent chocolate mousse.'

'How do you make such a thing?' I asked.

'Alice makes a very good whip, with eggs, butter, chocolate, icing sugar, cream and Cointreau,' proclaimed Miss Stein quickly, as if the intensity of our conversation had been but a moment.

'Ours are made with the addition of coffee, and are so light and creamy that they melt in the mouth,' the waiter pronounced in return.

'And how do you adorn them?' asked Miss Toklas suspiciously.

The waiter would not be outmanoeuvred.

'They are decorated with rosettes of whipped cream and chocolate leaves.'

The women smiled at me, as if enjoying this culinary competition, and I felt, for once in my life, that I actually belonged to a new family.

'Do you prefer whisky or Armagnac in a chocolate mousse?' I asked.

'Both must be at least ten years old, but I prefer the Armagnac,' the waiter observed solemnly. 'Although sometimes we add banana and rum.'

'The secret lies in the way you whisk the egg whites,' observed Miss Toklas.

'I agree entirely,' I broke in. 'The mountain peaks must be light and fluffy but contain a serious and aerated body.'

'But I think my favourite,' continued Miss Toklas, 'is a chocolate mousse with passion fruit sauce and raspberry cream.'

'I don't know,' said Miss Stein, sinking back into her chair. 'A mousse is a mousse is a mousse.'

I looked at the rose on the table between us and said nothing.

Suddenly Miss Stein reached out, clasped my hand and stared into my eyes.

'Say you love. Love what you love. Live with what you love.'

I did not know what to say in response.

'We are tired,' Miss Toklas told the waiter. 'We will take coffee in our room.'

The waiter bowed and withdrew.

'I must leave you,' I said reluctantly.

I was to be alone once more.

'What a pleasure it has been.' Miss Toklas held out her hand for me to kiss.

'I will never forget you,' I said, and indeed it was true. I think that I had never seen such love between two people.

'Repeat, repeat,' said Miss Stein. 'Go back, go back.'

I leaned forward to kiss her, but she waved me away. 'Back you must go. Back to when you last found happiness. Back to Mexico.'

I rose from the table, and walked past the remaining diners, clutching their brandies and their ports against their terrors and their fears.

As I reached the door, I turned to look back at the small wise woman and her ethereal companion for one last time.

'Thank you,' I said simply.

Miss Stein smiled, and said sadly: 'Love if you love. Live if you love. Love if you live.'

The *Mauretania* sailed into New York Harbor the following evening. Crowds of immigrants surged forward on the decks to have their first glimpse of the towering architecture before them: so much brick, iron and steel, and all so bold, magisterial and brave. Whereas I had previously found the natural terrain of mountain and sierra both humbling and daunting, it amazed me that humanity had found a means of competing with the environment, challenging its grandeur with an ambition of its own. It was as if a new scale of life had been invented, in which buildings would rise higher and higher and humankind would unwittingly, and at the very pinnacle of its achievement, make itself increasingly insignificant, dwarfed by its own creation.

We now sailed through a flotilla of small boats selling fresh water, poultry, bananas and rum, as the passengers on board set their sights on the land ahead, issuing great cries of '*Statua Liberta, Statua Liberta*'. It was the fourth of July and fireworks lit up the night sky, filling the air with hope and expectation. Those like me who had travelled in steerage were now taken on a ferry to Ellis Island where we were shown into a dark and cavernous building and ordered to line up for inspection.

It was a humiliating experience. Men and women were separated, families were dispersed, and the wait seemed interminable. The hall smelled of sickness. Children and adults alike began to sob with fear and anxiety, or looked bleakly across dark hallways, trapped in limbo between arrival and departure.

Guards asked us to strip and our clothes were removed for fumigation. Some people had letters of the alphabet chalked on their bodies if it was suspected that they had a poor heart, a hernia, a sexual infection or a mental illness. After I had taken a shower and been given a name-tag, my eyes were checked for cataracts, conjunctivitis and trachoma; my private parts were scrutinised for any signs of sexually transmitted disease, and my chest was inspected with a cold stethoscope, the doctor tapping away like a woodpecker.

Despite all my adventures it seemed that I had no more control of my destiny than when my travels had first begun. For I, Diego de Godoy, notary to the Emperor Charles V, who had first crossed the Atlantic as a glamorous conquistador, was now reduced to the status of immigrant worker waiting in line for an interview.

This proved to be a difficult encounter, for although the letter from my benefactor clearly put me at an advantage, the officials questioned why a Spaniard nearing retirement age (I think they took me to be a man of some fifty-six years old) should be indispensable to such a large organisation.

'Why do they want you, spic?'

'Spic?'

'Answer the question.'

'I know something of chocolate . . .'

250

I had been told to do nothing to annoy these people, no matter how provoking they became, because they controlled the destinies of thousands and could change a man's future with the sweep of a hand.

'You think the American people need a spic like you to tell us about chocolate?' the man continued.

'My benefactor seems to think so.'

'What's your name?'

'Diego de Godoy.'

'Age?'

'About fifty. I think.'

'Are you married?'

'No.'

'What is your calling or occupation?'

'Notary. No. Chocolate-maker.'

'I'm going to write Confectioner. Can you write?'

'Yes.'

'Have you ever been in prison or almshouse, insane asylum, or supported by charity?' the man continued.

'No,' I lied.

'Are you a polygamist?'

'No.'

At least I thought I wasn't.

'Are you an anarchist?'

'No.'

'Do you believe in or advocate the overthrow by force of the US Government?'

'No.'

'Are you deformed or crippled?'

'No.'

'Country of birth?'

'Spain.'

'Town?'

'Seville.'

The man met my eye briefly. Perhaps I would be arrested as some kind of impostor?

'On your way then,' the immigration officer said suddenly, and, it appeared, arbitrarily.

To this day I have never been able to anticipate the distracted moods of men at checkpoints. The officer even yelled after me, in a positively friendly manner: 'Don't forget to send me a few bars when you get there.'

'Sure,' I called back.

I had already begun to speak American.

Three days later I found myself at the gates of the factory in Pennsylvania.

The settlement had been built on its own rural site of one hundred and fifty acres and stretched as far as the eye could see. This was not the city centre community of Joseph Fry but an attempt at an earthly paradise where home and work were intermingled.

The town was dedicated to chocolate, with two main avenues named Chocolate and Cocoa signposting its importance; and with street names of Java and Caracas, Areba and Granada, it was impossible to escape the fact that the strange bean that I had first encountered with Ignacia was now responsible for the livelihood of an entire community.

There were houses with front lawns and back yards, toilets that flushed and showers that gushed, and it seemed that there was equal space for all. I felt as if I had entered a strange and fantastical utopia in which the threat of death had been removed.

Yet the factory for the production of chocolate was indisputably real. Here were machines for boiling, mixing, cooling, rolling, pulling, shaping, cutting, coating, and surfacing. There were instruments of which I had never heard: a triple-mill melangeur, a refiner conch, and a temperature controller. There were mould spinners, paste mixers, batch rollers, and enrobing machines; dryers, roasters, coolers, rotoplasts, crystallising machines, milk condensers, powder fillers and paste mixers. Women in white bonnets and white dresses sat behind batteries of dragée pans and sorting boxes, making chocolate in every form I could possibly imagine. Each stage of the process involved the employment of hundreds of people: cleaning and grading, roasting, blending, grinding, mixing, refining, conching, tempering, moulding, cooling, packaging and dispatching.

It was a veritable Camelot of chocolate.

Yet the actual taste was extremely strange. The milk was boiled on a low heat in a vacuum, and developed a curdled flavour: sour, unfamiliar and yet redolent of the odour of milk pails on the farm in Vienna. This did not seem to worry my American benefactor, who was convinced that he could sell such a heady creation 'in every five and dime store from Pennsylvania to Oregon,' but it did give me cause for concern, particularly when I was asked to assume the position of Director, Quality Control.

I was, at first, horrified. Determined to turn the job down, since I could not abide the taste of the bar, I remonstrated, as tactfully as I could, that my talents must lie elsewhere. I would rather inspect the original beans that arrived in our warehouse, checking each one for quality in order to ensure that, whatever the recipe, the finished product should be of the highest possible standard.

My benefactor, although surprised by my insistence on this, was mollified by my assurance that the quality of chocolate must always be dependent upon the nature of the original beans. And although I did not so much mind what he did to the cacao after it had arrived, I knew a good bean when I saw one, and am proud to say that we produced over one hundred thousand pounds of chocolate in the first year of my employment.

I had, of course, another reason for my desire to spend so much time inspecting beans, for much of the cacao was supplied by a certain plantation in Mexico.

Could my life turn full circle at last?

Each time I winnowed samples, or ground them in a pestle and mortar to check their quality, my dreams returned, and my head was filled once more with Ignacia.

I was a child, high up in a tree in the forest, and she was an old woman, making chocolate in the clearing where we had first known and loved each other.

She held up a chalice of chocolate and began to drink it, smiling strangely.

An enormous fire rolled over the top of the forest towards the hut.

I could sense the heat of the flames coming towards me.

A cacophony of distant voices shuddered on the wind and in the darkness, increasing in volume as they approached my ears.

Quien bien ama tarde olvida. The new love, the true love, the old love, the cold love. *Zwei Seelen und ein Gedanke. Vous pleurez des larmes de sang?* Two souls with but a single thought. *Liebchen, Liebchen. Querida. Querido mio.* Love knows no winter. *J'aime mieux ma mie, au gué, j'aime mieux ma mie. Das Leben ist die Liebe.* True love does not rust with age. Even the beautiful must die. *Tout passe, tout casse, tout lasse.*

Fire swept through the forest, blinding me, the voices rising and shouting, until it seemed to burn through me, tearing my insides, cleansing me with its scorching power, before moving on into the distance like a passing storm,

255

leaving only the blackened landscape remaining.

Yet Ignacia was still standing outside her hut, waiting for me, surrounded by blackness and devastation.

Her eyes were filled with sadness.

I knew that I could no longer imagine living without her. For this was what love meant to me now: a recognition of solitude, the need to be completed. *Al cabo de los años mil, torna el agua a su cubil.* At the end of a thousand years, water returns to its cask. We always return to our old loves. *I will see you again, amor mio; mis amores.*

Still within the dream, I now fell from the tree, hurtling towards the earth and awaking with a terrible shudder, as if I was a small boy again, alone after the death of my mother.

And then, perhaps more awake than I had ever been, I knew, for certain, that whatever happened, I would never find peace until I returned to Ignacia's grave once more. I could not believe that I could dream so vividly, or that the emotions I felt could have no value in my waking life. I even began to think that she was still alive: a living presence, a tangible memory. My heart could not accept the possibility of absence. I had to return to Mexico once more, even if it meant living by the grave. I could no longer tolerate this lingering existence of longing and despair.

I began to save as much of my earnings as possible, determined to leave as soon as I was able, to seek, once more, the woman I must love for ever.

'Well, I'll be damned.' My benefactor smiled benevolently when I told him. 'Why do you want to go there now?'

'To make things right. To redeem my history.'

'You want to find that girl?'

'I do.'

'After so long?'

'I will never be happy if I am far from her.'

'Your mind is certain?'

'Never more so.'

'I never heard anything crazier . . .'

'Or, I hope, more true.'

I stopped for a moment, uncertain as to whether I should continue. This man had been so generous to me.

'I cannot thank you enough for your kindness,' I continued.

'Well, you gave me the greatest idea.'

'Not me, my dog.'

'Ah yes! Your dog, God bless him.'

I reached out my arms and this great bear of a man hugged me to him, as if I had been the son that he had never had.

'I do not believe I can live alone any more,' I continued.

'I think you only understand love when you have lost it. If you can find it again, then there can be no greater happiness.' My patron smiled.

'I have met many people in my life, known hope, and tasted grief. I have tried to remember the events which have changed me and the beliefs to which I have stayed true. And I know now, that although I have enjoyed friendship, and tasted desire, I have only loved once. I must find that love again.'

My benefactor took my hand and shook it warmly for the last time. 'You are my very own knight of the doleful countenance. You deserve to find your Dulcinea.'

CHAPTER 12

I travelled in a trance of desperation, by railroad and by boat, in wagons and on foot, through Washington, Charlotte, Atlanta, Montgomery, New Orleans, and San Antonio until I reached Laredo and crossed the border into Mexico. Here I bought a horse and rode through the vast landscape of the Sierra Madre and on through Salamanca, Celaya and Acámbaro. A whole series of hallucinated cities blurred in the memory, just as if I was travelling towards Chiapas so many centuries before, as if my journey would never cease, until I finally arrived on the plantation where I had last seen Ignacia.

So much had changed, but when I saw the cacao beans and felt the heat of the sun against my face it was as if I had lost all of the four hundred years since I had been here last. I walked once more in the shade of the densely canopied trees and felt the weight and billowed softness of the fertile ground under my feet.

Some areas had been fenced off, and fierce security guards with thick moustaches and menacing dogs were on patrol. Seeing these animals made me think again of Pedro. How gentle he had been, how uncomplaining, how faithful.

Perhaps it was the thought of him that prompted the strangest of coincidences, for in the distance I saw a dark-coated lurcher with an uncanny look of Pedro about him.

The nearer I approached the closer the resemblance became.

I began to run towards the dog.

Thinking this a game, the lurcher ran far and away into the distance, until soon we were chasing each other across fields and track, through dense foliage and open glade, when we emerged at last, breathless and exhausted, into a vast and seemingly endless field of poppies.

'Pedro?' I cried.

The dog hesitated for a moment, but then ran on past a party of women who were making deep scratch marks in the poppy seed heads.

'Wait!' shouted one of the women, but I pressed on until I sensed the sudden approach of heavy footsteps behind me. Before I could turn to see who might be following, I was pulled to the ground and my hands were wrenched behind my back.

A gun was pointed to my head, and I was greeted with the words: 'Feel like dying?'

'Who are you?' asked a second man's voice. 'Why are you here?'

'I thought I had found my dog. He was lost.'

'Don't lie to me, punk.'

'It's true.'

'What are you doing in this field?'

'Don't hurt me.'

'Answer the question.'

I had no choice but to be honest, for my past had taught me that however fantastical my story might seem, further invention had only tended to make my trouble far worse.

'I was looking for a woman called Ignacia.'

'Who?' shouted one of the men, ramming what seemed to be another gun into my back.

It was impossible to reason with people I could not see and with my face so tightly pushed against the soil.

'Ignacia.'

'Do you know any women name of Ignacia?' I heard one ask the other.

'Ain't no Ignacia here.'

I felt a sharp blow to my head.

'Get up.'

I was hauled to my feet.

One of the men had a shaved head and a fierce demeanour. The other had, if such a thing were possible and I was not suffering the desperate delusions of the optimist, a more kindly disposition, and was chewing on a large green leaf that stained his teeth.

'She's not here,' said the fiercer of the two.

'You've got the wrong dog and the wrong woman.'

'Not doing so well, punk.'

'I am very sorry.'

'You know this is the Carlos plantation,' continued the bald man. A second gun gleamed in his pocket.

'No, I did not.'

'And you know what happens to scum who think they can get a little junk for free.'

'Junk?'

'Junk.'

Yet again a man was taking me for a lunatic, but I had learned by now that silence was the best course of action in order to avoid an antagonistic response.

'Scag,' the man continued, 'you know, smack, H, snow.'

Still I did not understand.

'Call it what you like,' said the man.

'All I did was follow the dog,' I began.

'Where are you from?'

'Spain.'

'No kidding?' said the man with the stained teeth.

'It's a long story. You won't believe me.'

'Try us.'

I took a deep breath.

The story of my life.

Again.

'It's about a woman.'

'The Ignacia chick.'

'I haven't seen her in a long time, and it's taken me an eternity to realise that I love her and cannot live without her.'

'When did you last see her?'

'Many years ago.'

'And you've come from Spain to find her? What she look like?'

I looked at the women working in the fields. Perhaps one of these might be her?

'Like no one else on earth,' I replied at last.

'Beautiful or ugly?' asked the fiercer of the two.

'She is beautiful.'

'She must have moved on,' said the contemplative guard.

'Quiauhxochitl. That was her name – in times long past,' I said, quietly.

'Quiauhxochitl?' said the fiercer guard. 'Isn't that the name of the *malinchista* in the canteen?'

'I don't think so.'

My heart missed a beat. Could she really be alive after all?

'You mean there's a woman called Quiauhxochitl in the canteen?'

'I think so.'

'Would she be about fifty years old, with long dark hair, and eyes of darkest amber?'

'That's the dame.'

My heart stopped.

I turned to the gentler of the men, desperately hoping for sympathy.

'And does she make the greatest chocolate you have ever tasted?'

'I'm not really a chocolate kind of guy.'

'I must see her.'

'No, man, no dice, no can do. You've got to leave our land and never come back.'

'No! I must see her.'

'We do not bargain, man. You're one lucky sonofabitch. We're letting you go.'

'Please. Let me find her,' I begged, stepping towards them.

'Get your ass away from my face.'

Had I come so far to leave now, with Ignacia so close and yet so unattainable?

'Sylvester, please. Don't talk to the gentleman like that,' the second man interrupted, before spelling things out to me in a more kindly manner. 'You gotta leave now without further questions. We're taking pity on you, because you talked about love . . .'

'And because getting rid of your dead body would be a considerable nuisance to us.'

I was in despair.

My life depended upon the outcome of this conversation.

'Let me just pick her some poppies, and give them to her.'

'Are you crazy?'

'Look,' I said, summoning all my feelings, in one desperate sentence, as if it was the last thing that I might say upon this earth. 'I don't think you understand. This is love. It is more important than anything in the world. It defines me. It is all I have and all that I want. If I cannot see her I would rather my life ended now. Shoot me if I cannot see her. Shoot me now and let me die rather than endure the torment of never seeing my love again.'

The men were silent.

'The disposal of the body would be a problem,' said the stronger of the two.

'I will dig my own grave for you,' I continued. 'But first, let me see if it is really her.'

The men stared at me.

'Do you like to gamble?' I asked desperately, remembering my reckless days in England.

They glanced at one another.

I kept talking, saying anything that came into my head, buying the time to persuade them to let me see Ignacia. 'Let me make this proposition. If she recognises me, then I will leave here now and live with her for ever.'

'And if she doesn't?'

'If she doesn't then I will walk with you to the very edge of your land. I will step outside your boundaries. I will write a note explaining my suicide. I will borrow your gun.'

'And then?'

'And then I will lie down in a grave dug by my own hands and kill myself.'

'Are you insane?'

'I have never been more serious. You cannot lose. You will either witness a passionate reunion or a grateful death.'

They paused, looking each to the other.

'I shall take silence as consent,' I continued, and

moved away into the field. 'I am now going to pick a small posy of poppies.'

'Only the flowers. Don't touch the heads . . .'

'I wouldn't dream of it.'

The men still seemed frozen to the spot.

'Help me,' I urged.

Hesitantly the two security guards now began to pick poppies by my side. The women in the fields continued their work, unaware of the drama unfolding before them.

I gathered a small posy and the two men, together with the intrigued dog (who had stayed by my side all this while), accompanied me to a low building in the distance.

I felt panic rising in me.

Was this the moment when Ignacia and I might be reunited? Perhaps I should warn her in some way, before she first set eyes on me? And what if she failed to recognise me? The encounter might be as empty and cold as my ill-starred reunion with Isabella all those years before. If so, then at least the comfort of death would be a merciful release.

I thought of what I might say to her – that love never tires, that it rules without laws, and that its power is determined by the strength our own hearts give it.

We arrived at the plantation canteen.

Sick with nerves, I pushed open the doors to the kitchen to reveal a sea of white aprons, gloves and hats amidst shining steel equipment. Dark chocolate revolved through the machinery around us, as if it had done so for all time.

Was she really here?

In the distance, a woman pulled off her hat and let her dark hair fall down onto her shoulders.

It was not Ignacia.

A second woman stared at me as if I had interrupted the most sacred of gatherings.

A third asked if she could help me.

Fear filled my being, and my head hurt so badly with the tension that I was worried that I would not be able to see.

I tried to focus on the far distance.

A woman in white was walking towards me.

Was this a dream?

The lady seemed to have a natural grace, unconcerned with the cares of the world as she carried a tray of newly made chocolate.

Then she stopped.

She looked about fifty-five years old, and was filled with beauty, sadness and wisdom; as if she had lived for all eternity and learned its secrets.

My God.

Here she was, extraordinary and unmistakable, *the woman that I loved.*

She looked up and smiled, as if she had been expecting me, as if she wondered why it had all taken so long, as if our reunion was the most natural thing in the world.

We looked across all the years of separation, across our dreams and our separate destinies.

'*Quien bien ama tarde olvida*,' I said. He who loves truly forgets slowly.

The workers looked on.

For a moment we simply stood there, staring at each other, as if we had done so for centuries, stupefied by love.

'I am sorry for all that I was when I first came here,' I began at last, 'and for all that I have done.'

She looked down at the floor as if suddenly shy, and then up, her eyes filled with tears, staring beyond me into the distance: into the past, and into the future.

I could not stop now.

'I regret the years that we have spent apart, the years when I did not know what love was. And I do not know how I have spent so many years without you.'

The chocolate machinery revolved around us like a lost constellation.

At last she spoke.

'*Querido. Querido mio.*'

'*Querida.*'

We walked towards each other and kissed.

The workers burst into applause, and we cried, silently holding each other as if we would never again be apart. I wanted time to stop then, and if it had done so I would have been able to bear eternity, for ever lost in that moment.

At last Ignacia whispered: 'I finish work at two o'clock. Wait for me in my house. If you would like . . .'

'How will I find it?'

'Felipe will show you.'

'Felipe?'

'My dog.'

'How can I wait so long now that I have found you?'

'It will seem short. Trust me.'

'Always,' I said and looked at the security guards over her shoulder.

'You're free to go, man,' said the fiercer of the two.

'Love carries its own reward,' added his more contemplative companion.

How did that time pass, in which I knew that I had found my love, but still could not be with her?

I determined to cook a feast that would welcome us back to each other: a meal filled with our past love, a banquet of memory and desire.

And so to the marketplace.

People were preparing for the Day of the Dead and the market had been overrun by skeletons. Children bit into skulls made of sugar, papier-mâché corpses toasted each other with tequila, and skeletal toreadors rested against gilded Madonnas on roadside altars filled with bread, flowers, candles and fruit. A skeleton mother gave birth to a skeleton baby aided by a skeleton doctor. It was a world where plenty met death in the face, filled with noise and colour, heat and dust, flowers and blood.

I found the familiar sights from four hundred

years ago, and as I looked into the faces of the people who stood beside stalls filled with oranges, pineapples, limes and lemons; chickens, partridges, quails and turkeys I could see the ghosts of their forefathers. So little had changed. Stout men and ample women stood by piles of plantains, pumpkins and papayas. An elegant woman sat behind a table of herbs selling not only cinnamon, aniseed and coriander, but also every kind of chilli – ancho, mulato, pasilla, chipolte, guajillo and cascabel. Two ladies poured *chocolate caliente*, which they whisked by rocking a wooden *molinillo* quickly between their palms. One man ate a handful of grasshoppers, while another laid coconuts out in the sun to dry.

Once again I was dazzled by plenitude. Colourful breads – *rosca de reyes* and *pan de muerto* – lay waiting in richly stocked *panaderías*. Groups of men stood smoking and drinking lemonade, red sorrel flower tea, pulque from fermented sap, *agua miel*, and freshly squeezed orange juice. There were enchiladas and enfrijoladas, steamed lamb tortillas filled with cheese, and tuna with roasted red pepper. I stopped by a stall selling thirty different kinds of *mole poblano*, and stood in wonder, remembering how far in the past I had first tasted such a delicacy. At the time it had seemed the most private, and the most beautiful moment in my life, and I could not imagine anyone else knowing of, or sharing, such things, but now all these delights were openly available, without need of preparation, for any who chose to select them.

And I felt that now my own life would have to open out in the same way. There could be no secrets any more, no hesitation. I would have to declare and stay true to my love.

I was filled with an urgent desire to tell Ignacia everything, to cook and to eat, to share at last our bodies, filled with love rather than lust, talking patiently and tenderly, yielding the secrets of the years in which we had been separated. It would be slow, gracious and generous, as we savoured our food and then our own flesh, together again at last.

But this was not the moment for reflection. I had little time, and was thrown back to reality by the task ahead.

I must cook the perfect meal. What could it be?

Ignacia would be home at two o'clock. Anything lengthy or complicated to create, such as lime-marinated red snapper with coriander, or even Antonio's wild hare in chocolate sauce would surely be impossible.

I began to seize the basic ingredients I needed in mounting panic.

Perhaps I could make it up as I went along?

No.

That would be the very worst way in which to behave. Had I spent all these years refining my skills only to abandon the notions of preparation, care and patience, the most basic elements that underlie all culinary ability?

And then it struck me.

Instead of one magisterial, unfolding banquet, surely it would be preferable to prepare a series of small plates, little delights which could be prepared for Ignacia to try at will, savouring each taste and flavour?

And so I gathered aniseed and avocado; chillies, cinnamon and chorizo; garlic, ginger, peppers, pumpkins, pulses and papaya; shrimps, scallops, limes, mangoes and maize, returning to Ignacia's house laden with so many good things that I staggered under the weight of them all.

'Home,' I said to Felipe the dog. 'Home.'

He led me to a small one-storey adobe dwelling with blue shutters at the end of a narrow lane. Filled with trepidation, I opened the door to Ignacia's house and set down my purchases.

There were four small rooms laid out before me: a pale-yellow living area with a reed sleeping mat, chairs, rugs, paintings and textiles, together with small pottery shrines and objects commemorating the Day of the Dead: the skeletons of priests, bishops, soldiers, judges, toreadors and angels, all made from painted clay. There was a tree of life, a miniature Ferris wheel, a series of glazed animals, even a box with a couple pledging eternal love: *Hasta que la muerte los separe.*

I then moved on to discover a tiled kitchen

filled with decorated plates, glazed bowls, *atole* mugs, utensils, and a wood-fired cooking area, over which was written *Mi casa es su casa*. There was a small shower area and a bedroom which I searched, jealously and fearfully, for evidence of the presence of any man.

It was clear that Ignacia, at least at this moment in her history, lived alone and in some comfort, far from the burned-out shell of a hut that I had envisaged in my dreams.

I would have to work fast to create the spread of delicacies I had in mind and began by preparing two different soups, vermicelli and gazpacho, placing the bread I had bought on a shallow wooden tray. Then I seared some cod with caramelised shallots, grilled calamari, and steamed the scallops with ginger. I marinated quails with rosemary, bay leaves and garlic, and lay guacamole between paprika-toasted potato skins. Stuffed green peppers with a walnut sauce were folded on dark green plates with pumpkin-blossom quesadillas. I filled a small earthenware casserole with a sizzling chorizo stew, spiked with sherry and coriander. Then I laid out bowls of peaches, figs and strawberries, and prepared a mango cream with almonds. The room was filled with the scents of cooking as I let the hot food rest in warm bowls around me.

I then took off my clothes, fearing briefly that Ignacia might return home and misinterpret my nakedness as peremptory, and plunged myself into a cold shower, washing away the heat of the market and the kitchen, towelling myself dry.

As I rubbed the towel against my neck, I caught the scent of Ignacia once more, heady musk rose and lily of the valley, and drank in the fragrance of her bathrobe. I could only hope that this would be my home at last, and that my troubled life might find peace.

Yet what could Ignacia be thinking? She had seemed so calm at the plantation. I could not believe that she did not think the same things as myself, but was incapable of imagining how she had passed the intervening years.

Sick with expectation, I could hardly contain myself as I dressed again.

Returning to the cooking, I tested each recipe, knowing that nothing must falter as the flavours rose around me. Then it struck me.

Flowers!

I hastily made an arrangement of blue poppies for Ignacia's table, and began to scatter poppy petals on her bed.

As I was doing so I heard Felipe's bark and the front door open.

'Diego!'

Ignacia's voice calling my name.

'What are you doing?' she asked as I emerged from her bedroom.

My hands were filled with petals.

'Welcome,' I said, stepping towards her.

Ignacia seemed reluctant to speak.

I knelt down and patted the dog. 'He looks so like Pedro.'

'He should do.'

'Pedro was his . . . ?'

'Yes. While we were in the glade.'

'Is Pedro . . . ?' She let the question fall away

'He is. He died in my arms.'

Again there was silence. This was not how I had imagined things.

'I've been cooking,' I said, abstractedly gesturing to the bowls that surrounded us.

'I can see. *Antojitos.*'

I smiled at her and put the poppy petals I was holding on the table.

'Ignacia,' I said softly, walking towards her.

Her face furrowed, and she looked fiercely into my eyes, stopping all movement. 'Why did you leave me alone for so long?'

'I came back. I looked for you – in Mexico and in Chiapas. I thought that you were dead.'

'How could I be? Did you think that I would have given you the drink without taking it myself?'

'But your grave?'

'I left it there in order to escape. It was all that I could do. They had to believe me to be dead. Did you not understand that?'

'It took me a long time to think what might have happened.'

'Did you not think of the things that I had told you? "If you are alive then I am alive. Never cease in your search of me."'

'Of course, but the grave . . . You could have come to Spain . . .'

'I did. I met a horrible woman, a cook . . .'

'Sylvana.'

'Yes. She told me the story . . .'

'And you saw Isabella . . .'

'She had no grace, no love in her heart.'

'Then how did you not find me?'

'You had left for Mexico, and by the time I returned you had gone to Chiapas, and then, by the time I had travelled there, you had vanished . . .'

'I have never not loved you,' I said softly.

'Nor I you.'

'Did you marry?'

'No.' She was shocked. 'I am not a *mala mujer*. Did you?'

'No . . .'

'There were others?'

'None that stopped me thinking of you . . .'

'I see.'

'I thought you were dead.'

Our love had survived centuries of war, accident and misunderstanding, but Ignacia was angry.

'Did it never occur to you that dissembling my death was the only way in which we could survive? I told you to trust me. "Love me. Never forget me. Never doubt me." You remember?'

'I remember everything; but there was so much devastation. It was war. I did not know that you could be so strong.'

'I thought the elixir could help us live a different

life, free of history, released from everything that might enslave us. I hoped that you would understand, that you would know.'

'How old are we?' I asked.

'I cannot be certain.'

'And will we die?'

'Oh, we are sure to die. Only we will have lived so much longer.'

'How much longer do we have?'

'I do not know. Perhaps ten years . . .'

'A hundred then . . .'

'Yes. Perhaps that is so.'

She seemed sad.

'Will you stay with me?' I asked.

'Let us eat,' she said, 'and talk. We do not need to say everything at once.'

I do not think that we were hungry, and we ate in silence, looking at each other nervously, as if we were frightened by happiness, unable to believe that we were together once more. We were too confused to appreciate the tortillas and the quails, the stuffed peppers, the chorizo, and the scallops. We were too excited even to speak.

I then asked if we could make chocolate together once more.

'You still have my *molinillo*?'

'I do.'

'I did not think that you would ever come,' she said softly. 'Are you much changed?'

'I hope that I am wiser,' I replied. 'I was afraid to return sooner. I did not know life well enough. I did not understand what had happened.'

'It has taken you all this time?'

'I am very slow.'

I reached into my bag and handed Ignacia the *molinillo*. 'Whatever we do, from now on, we will make our chocolate together. Here, in the place where we were last together.'

'Show me,' she replied, 'please.'

I did not think that I had ever felt so weary or so complete. It was as if all the cares of my past could be discarded as the incredible possibility of happiness stretched out before me.

We walked over to the fire, infusing the milk with vanilla, ready for the chocolate, the chillies and the cinnamon. I stood behind Ignacia, my arms around her, and we whisked the hot chocolate together.

'We have so much to say to each other,' I said.

'I used to think that we had all the time in the world,' Ignacia replied.

'No more.'

'No, no more.'

Ignacia looked back over her shoulder and smiled when she saw how adept I had become. But it was perhaps only when we finally poured out the mixture that our anxieties began to disappear and we knew that all might now be well, that we need no longer be alone or afraid in the world.

We took the chocolate into the bedroom, and drank slowly from the dark-red cups, savouring the taste.

At last Ignacia leaned over, and we kissed, simply, as if it was the most natural thing in the world.

Slowly, we began to take off our clothes, undressing one another.

'I am no longer young,' Ignacia said softly, frightened, more tentative even than when we had first been together. 'I am shy.'

The beaded blind rocked gently back against the window.

'Hush now,' I said, putting my finger to her lips.

Her soft breasts fell forward and I was amazed once more by their beauty. At last we lay down and began to touch one another carefully and tenderly, old worlds made new, pasts forgiven.

I knew now that the greatest kind of love comes when it does not matter who you are or what you have done. It does not matter if you fear the future or regret the past.

Everything is possible.

As we lay closely together a far-flung thunder rolled over the hills like a marimba. A street band struck up in readiness for the fiesta, firecrackers exploded in the sky, and the church bells began to ring. People were shouting in the distance and whistling, firing their pistols into the air, roaring as loudly as they could, as if to defy the inevitable silencing of their lives.

The Day of the Dead had arrived.

Quite soon it would be time for us to leave the

world. We would learn together how to love, and then, perhaps at last, how to die.

But not yet.

No.

Not yet.

ACKNOWLEDGEMENTS

Although this is a work of fiction, I am greatly indebted to several works of fact, most notably: *The True History of Chocolate* by Sophie D. Coe and Michael D. Coe; *The Conquest of New Spain* by Bernal Díaz (in which the Royal Notary, Diego de Godoy, is named); *Cortés: The Life of the Conqueror by His Secretary* by Francisco López de Gomara, translated and edited by Lesley Byrd Simpson; *Letters from Mexico* by Hernán Cortés, translated and edited by Anthony Pagden; and Thomas Gage's account of his visit to Chiapas in *The English-American: His Travel by Land and Sea.*

Fine recipes and wise observation on the nature of chocolate can be found in: *The Chocolate Bible* by Christian Teubner; *Chocolate: The Definitive Guide* by Sarah-Jayne Stanes; *The Chocolate Book* by Helge Rubinstein; and *The Complete Mexican Cookbook* by Lourdes Nichols.

For biographical information I am indebted to the excellent biography *The Marquis de Sade – A Life* by Neil Schaeffer; *Escape from the Bastille: The Life and Legend of Latude* by Claude Quétel;

and Simon Schama's magisterial *Citizens*. I have also benefited from *Freud, Biologist of the Mind* by Frank J. Sulloway, and Sigmund Freud's own *The Interpretation of Dreams*; while for the life of Gertrude Stein I have read not only her own work but also Diana Souhami's wonderful *Gertrude and Alice*. Back in America, I have been greatly helped by *Ellis Island Interviews* by Peter Morgan Coan and *The Emperors of Chocolate* by Joël Glenn Brenner.

As if this isn't enough, I must also thank the following for their kindness, tact, advice and patience: Juliette Mead, Georgina Brown, Jo Willett, Sue Stuart-Smith, Mark Brickman, Rachel Foster, and my daughters Rosie and Charlotte.

I am grateful for the attentions of my editors: Nick Sayers in London, and Sally Kim in New York, both of whom struck a constructive and encouraging balance between generosity and criticism.

But three people in particular helped me beyond all reason: the writer Nigel Williams, my agent David Godwin, and my wife Marilyn Imrie.

I cannot thank them enough.